Spirit Meadow

Also by Lauran Paine
In Thorndike Large Print

The Peralta Country
The New Mexico Heritage
The Horseman
The Homesteaders
The Marshal
Skye
Tanner

SPIRIT MEADOW

Lauran Paine

Thorndike Press · Thorndike, Maine

Library of Congress Cataloging in Publication Data:

Paine, Lauran.
Spirit meadow / Lauran Paine.
p. cm.
ISBN 0-89621-152-5 (lg. print : alk. paper)
1. Large type books. I. Title.
[PS3566.A34S6 1988]
813'.54—dc19 88-4934
CIP

Large Print edition available by arrangement with
Walker and Company, New York.

Cover design by James B. Murray.

Contents

Spirit Meadow

CHAPTER 1

A Meeting

At six thousand feet there were fir trees. Two miles lower down there was a mixture of red fir and pine, below that elevation at somewhere around three thousand feet, the firs thinned out and pines predominated: huge old rough-barked giants whose interlocking topmost branches had been all but closing out sunlight for hundreds of years. Where the sun did penetrate, it reached the forest floor in hazy shafts of light which made ideal camouflage for the big cats, bears and other meat-eaters whose domain this now was. A solitary rider on a muscular sorrel horse picked his way around trees and underbrush, thinking back to the Indians who used to own all this high country, and how they had probably had a wider selection of game to hunt than there was now. The reason he thought about the Indians was that since coming over the top-out at better than six thousand feet — above timberline — he had picked up a very old trail. In places it had been cut inches deep through solid rock where generations of Indians had passed.

He had seen no old camps, neither had he particularly looked for them. As a child he had heard how a series of redoubtable soldier-generals had rounded up the hideouts who had survived a hundred wild battles, and had herded them onto reservations. What he knew about redmen was no more than most other rangemen knew; they had left their fire-rings of blackened stone, their sunken circles where hide tipis had stood, and occasionally their askew old burial scaffolds. Otherwise, although he had encountered a few Indians, he knew very little about them.

But he knew cattle and horses, and men. At forty, anyone who had been living out of saddlebags for more than twenty years — or wintering in line camps, or nursing bruises from marking grounds — anyone who had followed the saddle-horseman's way of existence west of the Missouri River in which those three elements were constants, had learned right from the beginning that cows and horses could be outthought . . . and that a great many men could not.

His sorrel horse saw a sunny clearing on the right and changed leads as he looked over there. The rider pushed back off the saddle-fork and also looked. It was a nearly circular clearing, probably made long ago as the result of a fire started by lightning among the trees. Either rain, or lack of momentum, had let the blaze burn itself out before it consumed more timber.

Grass out there in the sparkling sunlight was stirrup-high. It had not begun to head out yet, as it was doing at lower elevations this time of year. The rider turned west but paused to sit a moment listening and looking, before passing out into the open country. The sorrel horse tugged his reins. The man let him have his head and they passed from speckled gloom to bright daylight.

It was a warm and beautiful glade. There was a piddling little creek on the far side which appeared to come from the far northern rims where snow lay in glazed layers year round. He dumped his saddle, draped the wet saddleblanket hair-side up to the sunlight, hobbled the sorrel horse, draped the bridle and turned slowly, looking in all directions. There was not a sound, except for a whisper over where the little coldwater creek ran. There was no movement either although clearly deer had been out here. He found their beds of smashed-flat grass.

The horse was greedily cropping grass. Later, he would be more discriminate and nip just the tops.

The man walked over to the creek and trout-minnows exploded in all directions as his shadow fell across the water. He got belly-down to drink, then arose wiping his beard-stubbled chin on a faded, worn shirt sleeve. By the position of the sun he thought it was about two o'clock in the afternoon. He had made good time. He gazed up at the forbidding, wind-scourged granite rims where he had picked his way very carefully across dirty old snow fields; it had been cold there but down here it was hot. He had been riding southward for seven days on his way to New Mexico. It occurred to him that this might be part of northern New Mexico.

He went back to his outfit, dug out the roll of fishline and returned to the creek. He had no luck with worms, but May flies lured enough fish for his supper. He thought again of the Indians who had surely fished this creek. Between their day and his day, a lot of speckled trout had come and gone. What lived in the little creek now knew nothing about men with snelled hooks. When he had cleaned enough fat fish for supper and breakfast, he left their offal in the grass and went back across the glade to set up a camp. He was not traveling on a schedule, so for the past seven days he had lingered wherever the living had been easy. He had a destination, but no set time to be there. And in fact while he had a name for the town where he was headed — Springville, New Mexico Territory — he had no directions for finding the place.

It was later, with the sun reddening in the west, that he went back among the pines for firewood, and it was while he was moving in zigzag fashion in his search that he encountered the bear tracks.

They were fairly fresh and deep in the needles. Tracks of a large bear. A man learned something about bears — and cougars, and wolves — if he'd spent most of his life in areas where they lived. Bears, for example, staked claims to territory. Outside of it, they would retreat before men. Inside of it, they would not retreat from anything they considered a trespasser, including men.

He went back to prepare an area for his little cooking fire, watched the grazing horse, and unfurled his blanketroll. He put the Winchester saddlegun beside it. As a solitary individual who was at home in this kind of an environment, he was relaxed and comfortable right up to the moment he heard the bear growl somewhere through the tall grass in the direction of the creek.

He stood up with the Winchester hanging slack in his right hand. His estimate of the beast's size had been correct, but what he had overlooked was a second set of tracks. They would not have been readily visible in pine needles anyway because the second bear was a cub. The large bear was an old sow, sleek and larded and scarred. She had found those fish entrails and was sharing this treasure with her cub.

At a fresh sound he turned to his left. The sorrel horse had picked up bear scent and was as rigid as a stick, although as yet he had not seen the bears. But he was looking for them. Wolves and mountain lions inspired instant dread in horses, but bears terrified them, in part no doubt because bears, as carrion eaters, smell much worse than either big cats or wolves.

The old sow was sitting on her backside, rearing back slightly so her cub could eat. She evidently was not hungry. But she had only one interest — her cub — and when a light breeze blew from the west she immediately detected the horse smell and the man scent.

For the thick-shouldered, beard-stubbled man in his faded britches and old butternut shirt, there was nothing to do but wait. Everything was up to the old sow. If she thought the scent was faint, which would mean the horse and man were not close, she might be content to herd her baby back across the creek and into the timber.

The man watched, remained absolutely motionless, and waited. Bears have poor eyesight, therefore at a distance she would act or react according to movement. He did not move, nor did his horse.

He had plenty of time to study her and one thing stood out: she had ragged ears and many scars, and like most bears, she would have an unpredictable temperament. Judging from those scars the man suspected that even if she had not had a cub, she would not have retreated with good grace. With a cub, which makes all sow bears fiercely protective, and with her obviously aggressive nature, she might not withdraw toward the timber — she might start following the alien man smell toward what she perceived as a threat to her baby. Anything as powerful as a bear weighing upward of eight hundred pounds had no reason to fear opposition of any kind — except men. But that was a dim instinct at best, and it might be that this instance neither inherent caution nor instinct would prevail. To this sow, the cub alone mattered.

The sorrel horse had exhausted his courage and began to fidget, then hopped in the direction of the man. The bear immediately detected movement and the man turned disgustedly toward the sorrel and said, "Now look what you did."

The sow stood up to her full height. She was head and shoulders taller than the man who was watching her. She tipped her face and sampled the air, then growled and sank back to all fours. The cub was finishing his repast of offal and nothing else interested him until the sow gave him a rough cuff in the direction of the creek. He squealed sharply, then sat down to whine bitterly.

The man watched the sow put the cub behind her as she squared around facing ahead, jaw slack, flat head weaving slightly as she began her shambling, pigeon-toed advance, growling intermittently as she came.

The man spoke to the horse without taking his eyes off the sow. "Damn you, Red."

The horse was shaking like a leaf. He had rocked back so that all his weight was on his haunches. He was prepared to lift his hobbled front legs, whirl, and hop in terrified retreat faster than he had ever hopped before.

Without haste the man raised his saddlegun, snugged it back and settled the old sow's right-shoulder area between buckhorn sights drawing her to him for the shot.

Back on the creekbank the cub was wailing to high heaven as he got over onto all fours and began loping to catch up with his mother. He very suddenly halted and swung back toward the creek. Whatever had diverted him had no effect on the man or the advancing old fighting sow. Each of them was serious. Dead serious.

The sow was beginning her plunging, loose jointed gallop, the final phase of her charge, when she suddenly stumbled, growled and tried to reverse direction so fast that she fell in a writhing heap. With both front paws she swatted at something the man could not see. She rolled and roared, batting behind her.

The man, whose finger had been taut inside the trigger-guard, scarcely breathed. The sow got to her feet and like a dog chasing its tail, went round and round. Now, the man saw blood on her flank, and then the arrowshaft sticking upright from one of her hams. He was too dumbfounded to move for several moments, not until the old sow turned back in anguish toward her cub, that wood shaft bobbing as she fled.

The man slowly grounded his saddlegun as

the sow collected her cub, and while occasionally twisting to swipe at the arrowshaft, splashed into the creek, up the far back and still roaring, disappeared through the distant trees.

Finally now, with one peril survived, he stood motionless, searching the shadowy distant timber for what was probably another peril. The hair at the back of his neck was stiff. The sorrel horse still quivered but was no longer poised to whirl and flee. The man spoke to him again, something he'd been doing for several years and as usual the horse paid no attention. He said, "Now you got somethin' to sweat about. That arrow didn't come from the moon." He paused, peering intently into the middle distance, and still saw nothing as he continued, "And you can bet he's got more than one arrow."

The sorrel horse dropped his sweaty neck to snatch at grass heads, then raised it very quickly, little ears pointing, nostrils distended. But this time he was not terrified, he was wary because that was his nature. Mostly, he was curious.

Long after the sound of the sow and her cub crashing through underbrush had faded, a spotted horse bearing what appeared to be a wizened, weathered, elfin-sized Indian appeared in the sunlight with forest gloom at his back. The spotted horse halted in response to pressure on a squaw-rein as his oddly attired rider sat motionless and silent, studying the man out in the middle of the mountain meadow.

The silence ran on until the man standing with his sorrel horse decided whoever the stranger was, he was not an immediate threat, otherwise the old man would have let fly another arrow. He raised an arm, palm forward. He could have spoken but he didn't. There were usually language barriers between people of different cultures, but a palms-forward salute seemed to be universally understood.

The rider urged his spotted horse across the creek, raised his own right arm on the far side, and walked his horse straight toward the man beside the sorrel horse.

CHAPTER 2

Hawk's Story

What made the wizened, bronzed old man appear even smaller than he was, was his mount. The spotted horse was at least sixteen hands tall. He was muscled-up, young and with the good eyes of a sensible and dependable animal.

The horse was wearing an Indian saddle with the high fork in front and back. It was also carrying a handsome silver engraved Spanish bit with elaborate cheekpieces, but there was only one plaited horsehair rein.

The rider was not much taller than five feet, and judging from his wrinkled, narrow, blue-eyed face with its broad lipless mouth, he was certainly not less than sixty years of age and could be a lot older. His movements were quick, decisive and birdlike. He had an old hunting rifle and wore an old long-barreled six-gun with a walnut handle worn smooth and shiny with age and use.

The small man's trousers were split-hide

doeskin, as soft and pliable as silk. There was no Indian fringe, but there were greasy creases and many stains. Like the shirt, which was of the same material, the trousers had not been washed in a long time, showed the ravages of hard use and the signs of many careless meals after which greasy fingers had been wiped on them. The old man had a gut-strung stubby bow and a parfleche of arrows.

Invisible to the younger man was a circle of white beads on the back of the shirt about twice the size of a man's palm. In the center of the white circle was a bear's paw in dark red beads — the symbol of hunting prowess.

As the men smiled at each other the taller, thicker and younger man wagged his head and said, "I didn't want to kill the old fool."

The answer he got was in clipped English but without any accent. Evidently English was the dark old man's first language. "I didn't want you to kill her. Not with a cub too young to get along without her." Two close-set hard blue eyes flicked around the little camp and jumped back to the younger man's face. "You got plenty trout for the both of us?"

The rangeman nodded. "Creek's full of 'em. We can get more for breakfast. My name is Joe Bryan."

The old man lifted his greasy, shapeless old hat, scratched vigorously, reset the ancient hat, and bobbed his head like a little old bird. "Joe Bryan . . . My name is — I got several. Call me Hawk. That's close enough. You traveling through, Joe?"

"Yes. Heading down for New Mexico to look up a town named Springville."

The small old man's dark eyes widened on Joe and remained very still for a moment. Then he said, "Well, if you want to set the fire, I got to go back across the creek; then I'll be back." The old man abruptly turned toward his tall spotted horse.

Joe was curious about how so small an old man would get atop such a tall horse. The old man did not turn the stirrup to toe into it. He gathered his squaw-rein and sprang off the ground, hit the stirrup with his toe and swung his right leg over the saddle. Joe Bryan had seen men do that before, but never one as old as Hawk appeared to be.

He watched Hawk and the large horse go back to the creek and splash across it. The old man could have friends over there in the dark forest. Joe shrugged and sank to one knee, and began gathering dry twigs for their supper fire. The sorrel horse had hopped back out where the grazing was ideal and did not even appear to remember the bear.

The sun was far off-center to the west and like summer suns, it was reddening as it sank, but there would be several more hours of daylight. In fact long after the sun had departed there would still be daylight at this time of year.

And it would turn cold. At this elevation it would be cold in the forest, even at the height of summer. Lower down and beyond the timber, it would be hot enough to fry eggs on a rock almost any time of day, and nights would not be a whole lot cooler. There was much to recommend a big, high-country meadow like the one Joe Bryan had decided to spend a few days in before heading down out of the mountains.

He watched the shadows form beyond his meadow and eventually cross it. He was ready to start frying trout and looked west across the creek for sign of the bronze-skinned little old mountainman. By the time he saw the spotted horse emerge from forest darkness he was hungry enough to eat the tail end of a snake if someone was around to hold its head.

Hawk came across the shadowy meadow, and to Joe Bryan in that kind of other worldly light he looked like something out of a myth. A bizarrely attired *fantasma*.

Joe slapped two big trout into his iron fry pan and stirred coals beneath it as Hawk came up, swung off and without a word sank down to hobble his horse before stripping it of its riding gear. That was when Joe saw the white circle on the back of the old man's buckskin shirt, with the red bear paw in the middle of it.

Hawk came over and squatted. "You got any whiskey by any chance?"

Joe shook his head. "Ran out a week back."

Hawk watched the frying trout and inhaled deeply. "Week back? You been on the trail that long?"

"Yep. From Colorado."

"Rangerider?"

"Yep."

Hawk paused to watch Joe turn the fish, then spoke again. "Last time I set with someone like you was about nine years back. Outlaw that time. Said his name was John Smith an' he needed directions to the Messican border. Nice young feller, but nervous as that snake was in the Garden of Eden."

Joe put one large trout on a tin plate, the only plate he owned, handed it over, and ate the other fish from his fry pan. "That's a long time not to talk to anybody," he said. The trout was delicious — or Joe was just hungry as a bitch wolf.

Hawk ate half his fish before speaking again. "You been married, Joe?"

He eyed the old man thoughtfully. He had been raised to never ask direct, personal questions. He did not do it and he did not appreciate having other people do it. But Hawk was not just anyone. Whatever he was — or had been — judging from the looks of him, he had lived a long, probably very colorful life; and if, as Joe suspected, he had spent a lot of time among Indians, who had no such inhibitions, it probably did not occur to him that he was being rude.

Joe shook his head. "Nope. Never have. Never figured I could afford it. Anyway, it's too late now."

Hawk's head came up quickly, with that birdlike movement which seemed characteristic of him. "Too late? You're still a pup."

Joe wryly smiled. "Forty last spring, Hawk."

"Forty, for Chris'sake! When I was forty I could do anythin' I'd done at eighteen. Forty!" Old Hawk snorted his derision of any such preposterous notion as a person being old at forty. "Dump couple more fish into the fry pan, Joe. How long's it been since you ate?"

"This morning."

"Me, I haven't ate since yesterday morning."

Joe's eyes twinkled. "You been runnin' from someone, Hawk?"

The old man did not even glance up. "In these mountains? Joe, I been fifty years in here, from one end to the other, from Wyomin' south to down here in New Messico. I never had to hide. I just sort of turned to stone and let 'em ride right past me." Hawk's head snapped up, his pale eyes were fixed on the younger man and he cackled with laughter. Then he said. "Joe, 'bout the time you was straddling diapers I was sittin' on lookouts with Indians I'd known many years watchin' soldiers combin' the hills for hideouts. It was like watchin' ants over a carcass. They stumbled and cussed and sweltered and got hurt, then sat with their faces to bright supper-fires and their backs exposed, like little chil'ren." Hawk paused to watch memories writhe in the firelight flames. After a pause and in a softer voice he said, "There was too many of 'em. Hunnerds. Some'd get shot, some'd go back, others would take their places. It was like tryin' to beat back a flood." Hawk turned to watch the next pair of trout fry and shook himself.

Joe watched the fry pan's contents too as he said, "Bad."

Hawk raised his eyes to study Joe's face a moment, then nodded, and changed the subject. "Springville, eh? You know where it is?"

"Nope. Just that it's in New Mexico."

"Well now, Joe, when you leave this meadow you go back west to the trail and turn direct south. You'll come out'n the trees about five miles down. Then you'll cross a big grassland country that belongs to a mean old bastard named Campbell. Big cattle outfit. You cut diagonal to the southeast — you payin' attention?"

Joe laughed. "I'm payin' attention."

"All right. Cut diagonal southeast and along about tomorrow evening you'll see it. Cowtown with log buildings, nice big old trees from back when it was a tradin' post." Hawk accepted the tin plate with his second trout on it. He ate with a wicked-bladed belt knife with a worn-smooth horn handle. "Wouldn't do no good for you to tell me who down there you want to see because I haven't set a foot in Springville since they changed its name from Buffalo Camp. Anyone I knew down there forty years back is dead by now."

Joe ate fish and accepted the fact that without any idea of how he had managed it, he had entered New Mexico Territory just about where he would have planned to, if he had known what part of the area Springville was in.

A slight chilly breeze arrived from the west. It made a sad, forlorn sound as it came out of the timber on the far side of the little creek, and Joe stopped chewing to raise his head because borne upon the little vagrant breeze was a sound as though someone were crying. It was very faint and it stopped as the wind changed course and began bending grass from the north.

Hawk was watching the younger man as Joe turned to face him. The old man said, "You hear something?"

"Yes. Sounded like someone crying."

Hawk's little shrewd eyes narrowed and his wide lipless gash of a mouth tipped upward at the outer edges. "They're out there, Joe."

"Who is out there?"

Hawk sucked his fingers, tossed the bones from the tin plate and pulled a swatch of grass to scour the plate with before replying. "There was a rancheria in this meadow. I lived in it for a couple years, then went north to trap beaver with some Indians from here. We was gone three months in the wintertime. When we come ridin' out of the trees over yonder — about where I come out from today — everything was gone. Horses, people, dogs, all gone. The hide tents had been dragged into a pile and burnt. . . . We had a wailing time, then we buried what the varmints hadn't dragged away to gnaw on.'

Joe was motionless. "What happened?"

"Massacre, Joe. It wasn't just soldiers. It was mostly their scouts and camp robbers. 'Breeds from the settlements, scalp hunters, scum of the frontier." Hawk wiped greasy fingers on his trouser legs. "Mostly, they had nothin' against tribesmen; they wanted their horses and weapons and jewelry, anythin' they could plunder. . . . It's all down there in the ground under the grass, the burnt remains and the graves. We didn't dast make burial platforms. Scavengers used to plunder them to steal whatever was buried with the Indians — weapons, blankets, iron pots, jewelry. We buried 'em white-man style, in the ground, then we dragged out any sign there was graves." Hawk gestured casually. "This here is Spirit Meadow. They're out there."

Joe used grass to clean the fry pan and packed away his little salt sack and pepper tin, using saddlebags because he had no *alforjas* — he did not own a pack animal. Then he hunched a little to feed more dry twigs into their dying fire. The cold was increasing but the wind had stopped.

He was quiet so long old Hawk went to his saddle and returned with a soiled heavy blanket which he wrapped himself in and sat across the little fire looking more than ever like something out of dim history: expressionless, wizened, hands like monkey paws clutching the old blanket, calculating gaze fixed on the thick, powerful, hunched body of the younger man opposite him.

Joe eventually looked up and met Hawk's appraising stare. Red-orange embers highlighted the bony parts of the old man's face; darkness filled the lower places. The result was an image of something human, yet not human — with faint tendrils of smoke passing in front of it, and the shifting light of orange coals altering planes and angles where there was no expression at all.

Hawk said, "I had two pups an' a squaw. Young she was an' as pretty as a speckled bird. . . . She's buried here along with our little boy. . . . The little girl, she was three years old, they took her away with 'em. Sold her to a Messican family. By the time I found her she was married to a trader. She traveled with him. His name was . . . It don't matter. She died ten days back. . . . Joe, I'm goin' to roll in. . . . We got enough fish left for breakfast? I wake up hungry. Always have."

"Hawk — don't lie awake. There are six fish wrapped in the grass."

The old man stood up clutching his blanket. "I don't lie awake. You sleep good, Joe. I'm glad I come onto you. I think you're a good man an' I like you."

CHAPTER 3

Riding Double

False dawn arrived and it was bitterly cold when a god-awful howl brought Joe upright in his bedroll with a pounding heart. The sound was very close. He was fumbling for his six-gun even before his mind had cleared.

Where Hawk should have been inert in the grass there was not even an outline. Joe swung his head. His sorrel was out there, a dim but recognizable silhouette in the pale gray new day. But there was no sign of the spotted horse.

Another of those screeching howls shattered the utter hush of premorning in the meadow. Joe was wide awake as he shook out of the blankets, stood up and looked downward and around through the tall grass.

He saw some movement, but in the poor light thought it was either a badger or polecat and let his gaze continue to search out the source of those howls. It could not be anything very small to make that much noise. As he stepped away from the blankets to widen his search area, another great scream to his left and behind brought him around with his gun raised. There was no seven-foot-tall bear, there was not even a crazy old wolf. The noise had come from that struggling bundle in the grass, so he pushed through and stopped dead still in his tracks. The bundle did not appear to have an opening but there was definitely something inside it that was very upset and active. Joe pushed the bundle with his foot. Immediately all the writhing stopped and there was not a sound.

Joe pushed it again. A human sound like a whimper came out and Joe sank to one knee with a bad premonition. He looked up once, over in the direction of the creek, then reached to lift away some of the wrapping.

A child with dark eyes, dark hair and a tan-golden complexion stared straight up at him. One small hand caught hold of one of Joe Bryan's fingers and clung with surprising strength.

Joe put up his six-gun, slowly looked back toward the creek, then had his attention pulled back by a muffled but distinguishable whimper. The clutching small hand had been joined by its mate as the small child tried to pull itself into a sitting position.

Joe saw a tiny red shirt and faded blue trousers, both very dirty. The child was barefoot. Joe hoisted the small blanket around the child's shoulders, then he raised his head again, looking for movement, saw none and yelled loudly. "Hawk, you damned old scoundrel, you come back an' get this kid!"

He did not expect an answer and he particularly did not expect to see the tall spotted horse appear, but he had to yell at someone, or something.

The shout startled the child, who clung harder and began to cry softly as it pulled hard to rise off the ground. Then the child released Joe's hand and clung to him with sturdy small arms around his neck.

Joe instinctively responded to the unsteady legs with a hand against the child's back to support it as he glared toward the creek and muttered, "You old son-of-a-bitch."

Daylight was coming. Joe took the child to his scorched cooking area, bundled it against the cold, put wood scraps atop some coals and got down on all fours to blow heartily. The child's dark eyes watched. When Joe got some smoke started and fanned with his hat for the fire to follow, the child laughed. Joe looked around but did not even smile. Some other time he might have been able to see the humor in a grown man's rear end sticking up in the air while his head and shoulders were on the ground as he blew into ashes, but not today.

When the fire was blazing, Joe went after his hat, boots and jacket, then he too sat hunched in front of the heat. The sun arrived as it commonly did this time of year; one moment it was not out there, the next moment it had come up over the horizon like a seed being popped out of a grape.

Joe blew out a big breath and turned. He knew nothing about children except that they were small. The child looked back at him with equal gravity. Then it offered a timid little smile and Joe said, "Well, hell . . . I hope you like fried trout." He paused in the act of unwrapping the grass around yesterday's catch. "You don't live on milk do you? Because if you do, we're in one hell of a fix."

The child did not respond. It simply, sat inside the dirty little blanket watching everything Joe did.

It was a meager meal, the kind Joe was accustomed to. He had used up his small bag of coffee two hundred miles ago, and his baking power and flour for biscuits as well. When he offered the child a cooled-off and deboned golden-brown trout on the tin dish, it reached with both hands. Apparently, the child was famished.

Joe's appetite was a lot less than it should have been as he watched the child wolf down food. He said, "You can't talk, eh? Well, that'll most likely mean you're not old enough yet. But you can sure eat. . . . I wish I had that old goat by the neck right now. . . . Damned old scoundrel . . . That's the crying sound I heard last night. He had you over yonder hid out in the timber. That's what he went back over there about when I was readying to cook supper."

Joe had fried another trout for himself, but when the child looked up, he slid that fish onto the tin plate too. There were still two unfried trout but Joe had no appetite at all as he watched the child and growled to himself. "What's your name? . . . Oh hell, forget it. It's beginning to dawn on me who you are. He said his daughter died ten days ago. . . . I'll bet a new shirt you are his daughter's kid and that confounded old monkey stole you and ran for it. . . ."

The child put the tin plate aside in the grass and methodically wiped greasy hands on its old blanket. Joe said, "Don't do that. Here, use my bandana." He bent over to wipe the child's face first, then put the bandana in its hands. The child smiled up at him.

"Oh gawd damn," he muttered and sank down beside the child to build up the dwindling fire. An afterthought made him reach for his canteen, uncap it and hold it so the child could drink. It took on nearly as much water as a grown man would have done. Then, before Joe had even put the canteen aside, it edged sideways, put its head in his lap, made a little puppy-sound and closed its eyes.

Joe extricated himself gently, covered the child, made a low pillow for it from one of his bedroll blankets, scuffed the fire with a boot toe, and left the camp. He walked stiffly out where the sorrel horse was picking grass heads which were made particularly flavorful by dew.

He glared at Red. The sorrel horse cast one indifferent look in his direction and resumed picking grass heads. Joe said, "Red, did you see that little phantom go riding off on his big spotted horse last night? Why didn't you nicker? Any other time you nicker. You know what he did — that dried-up little old brown prune? He had that all figured right from the time when he shot that sow bear in the butt to get her away from our camp. He had that child hid out in the trees. When it cried and I heard it he made up a story about ghosts of dead Indians. . . .

"Red, I can't imagine why he'd steal his dead daughter's child. He said she was married to a trader so it's got a father somewhere. . . .

"By golly he never mentioned any names. Just one — Hawk. I'll bet you my first month's wages when we hire out again that every third or fourth Indian out here is named Hawk. . . . What do we do with the little kid? I don't know how old it is. It's no more'n a handful in size and it can't talk. But it sure can eat. . . ."

The sorrel horse rolled up his top lip to work loose packed grass stalks.

Joe looked on in disgust. "Yeah. Funny as hell isn't it? I should know better than to talk to you." He turned back toward the fire. A hundred and fifty yards northward was a prime wolf, twice as large as a dog, working a scent which took it back and forth through the grass. The wolf was slick and silvery, with a shading of white on his face. He was on a breakfast scent and apparently had failed to see the man farther out, who had stopped stone-still to watch him.

It could have been the fragrance of cooked fish that had brought the big wolf this close to a place where there was also horse scent and man scent. He had to be very hungry; normally wolves would not approach within a mile of men. Joe guessed the air was not drifting from him up to the wolf. As he watched, the big animal crept closer to the camp and the sleeping child. Joe abruptly came to life and yelled. The wolf froze. Joe starting running and waving his hat at the same time.

The wolf did not give ground for a while, not until Joe was within a couple hundred feet of his camp — and his Winchester — then it whirled and loped with long strides in the direction of the northward timber.

Joe burst through the tall grass and dived for his carbine. The wolf was beyond range. The danger was past but Joe still gripped the Winchester. When the wolf finally disappeared, he lowered the gun and leaned on it. The child was sleeping like something in hibernation. Even the shouting had not wakened it.

Joe arose, put the gun aside, spat, ran bent fingers through his hair, reset the hat and pitched more wood onto the fire. It was still early, and cold.

He sat down near the fire and looked at the sleeping child with its soft expression of innocence and helplessness, wagging his head. "That damned old sly-faced grandfather of yours ought to have his backside kicked all the way up to his shoulders."

The sun climbed, warmth reached Spirit Meadow, and Joe tried to imagine how he'd look after a small child up here. He decided he had better strike camp, rig out and head for Springville. His sister lived down there, which was why he had been on his way in the first place. They had not seen each other in something like ten years. She was all the family he had and she had written him last autumn at a place called Tie Siding north of the Colorado line over into Wyoming, inviting him to New Mexico for a visit.

His sister had no children although she had been married to a man named Wes Turner for twelve years. Childless or not, she would know what to do with Hawk's grandson — or daughter. Women just naturally knew things like that.

He looked at the sleeping child. It was sweating, so he gently removed a blanket and used his bandana to wipe perspiration off its face. Which was it? It had to be one or the other, and of course there was a very simple way to find out, but instead of checking, he arose abruptly to go look at his horse equipment. Damned if he would do *that*. Anyway, as soon as he could find his sister he'd be rid of the child, so whatever it was did not matter.

What kind of an old discard from another era would abandon a child, for gosh sakes? The answer was not difficult to find: exactly the kind old Hawk was.

He had everything ready before wakening the child. It sat up groggily. Joe held the canteen and it drank, then smiled up at him. He could tell it needed a good scrubbing at the creek, but that would have to wait until they reached Springville.

They headed west out of the big meadow, the child clinging to him behind the cantle, evidently experienced at this sort of thing. Joe Bryan looked back once, then rode into the forest gloom thinking that if whatever else lay ahead in New Mexico was to be anything like his first encounter here in Spirit Meadow, his visit in Springville would be very short.

The sorrel horse found the old trail without difficulty and instinctively turned southward. Heat penetrated the forest the lower they went. When it was possible to see open grassland through the trees, the sun's glare in the open country had Joe Bryan squinting for a mile before he left the slope and rode out onto a huge mesa. The range country seemed to be encircled by mountains, most of them so distant that even through pure sunlight they looked like blue-blurred, crumpled brown paper.

He followed old Hawk's directions, aiming southeast, and saw no buildings although Hawk had said there was a large cow outfit down here somewhere. But he saw cattle, most of them half wild and willing to run at sight of him, tails up over their backs like scorpions. He saw several bands of someone's loose stock, but they fled at sight of him also, and being horses, covered a lot of country more swiftly than the cattle had.

He was a rangeman, with a rangeman's interest in new territory. He forgot about the child while admiring the grass, the bigness of the country, the little veiny creeks that provided water for livestock, and occasional bosques of trees where animals could den up for shade this time of year.

The child whimpered and clutched at his shirt. Joe halted and twisted around. The little sweaty face was looking up at him in mute desperation. Instinct told him what the problem was. He swung off, lifted the child down, and in the shade of the sorrel horse nodded as he said, "All right. Go right ahead and take care of it."

The child reached for his fingers as its lips

began to quiver. It tugged at him. The sorrel horse looked around in response to the little puppy-sounds.

Joe freed his hand and unslung the canteen even though he did not believe thirst was the problem. It wasn't; the child refused to drink and seemed unable to stand still. Joe replaced the canteen, saw the horse watching him, and snarled at it. "Mind your own business."

He knelt to fumble with a rope belt. The child stood patiently waiting. Joe had not quite finished when the child could restrain itself no longer. Joe moved but not fast enough. He stood up fishing for his bandana, eyeing the child with disapproval. But a minor mystery had been cleared up. The child was a boy.

They were astride again when a large eagle came soaring overhead to satisfy its curiosity. Joe felt the child cringing against him behind the cantle and said, "It's all right. It won't hurt you."

The eagle made several spirals, steadily sinking lower, then, having satisfied himself about what was below, moved powerful wings to gain altitude. As the eagle flew southwesterly, the child's grip on Joe's shirt in back eased up. Joe said, "I told you — he wouldn't hurt you. Now if you'd been a squirrel or a rabbit . . ."

He let it trail off into silence. There were times when he got more response from the sorrel horse than he ever got from the child.

There was nothing to hold his attention after he had made a favorable assessment of this country he was crossing, so his mind returned to old Hawk. Last night by the campfire Hawk had asked if Joe had ever been married. Maybe that should have warned Joe that Hawk had something devious in his mind, but it hadn't.

The child squirmed again. This time Joe's response was to fish in a saddlepocket, pull out a lint-encrusted, crooked stick of jerky which was as brown and tough as rawhide, and poke it into the child's mouth. The squirming stopped. In its place there were loud, wet sucking sounds. Joe shook his head and squinted toward the flat skyline. Hawk had said he would see trees and rooftops by evening.

Right now evening seemed an awfully long way off. He dug out another stick of jerky and chewed this one himself. It never took the place of real food but it was better than nothing.

CHAPTER 4

Open Country

The final stop before they got near the town was alongside a shallow little warmwater creek which had lacy willows lining both banks. According to the position of the sun it was about three in the afternoon, and although the heat was high, there was shade beside the creek, and coolness. The child had gradually loosened his grip on Joe's shirt in back. Joe had noticed, had waited until the small hands dropped away, then he swung in the saddle and caught the falling child.

Now, as he hobbled the horse and pulled off its rigging so it could graze, the child slept in soft grass without even moving a finger. It did not occur to Joe that small children took naps. He assumed that since the child had not slept well last night it required sleep now. In fact, with the sorrel drowsing and the child sleeping — and no real reason to hasten now that he thought the town could not be very distant — Joe scuffed the soft earth to be sure there were no snakes, then settled comfortably, tipped down his hat and relaxed. Within a minute he too was asleep.

The sun continued its downward slide, casting faint smudges of shadow among the willows. Nearby, creekwater rippled softly over rocks, and the blessed coolness of this particular area would probably have induced drowsiness in a rock.

Birds returned to the willows where some had nests and others roosted because the creek banks' soft earth had worms as well as insects in abundance. Joe heard nothing, not the creek, the birds, not even the grunted expressions of surprise as a topless light buggy came along. The buggy was accompanied by a rangy, rawboned, darkly tanned horseman who had a hint of gray above his ears.

"Saddle tramp," explained the rawboned saddlehorseman, looking with disapproval at Joe Bryan's flat-out and motionless form.

The equally astonished driver of the topless buggy had flattened lips, a slightly beaked nose, hard gray eyes and a bun of coiled gray hair at the nape of her neck. She looked first at Bryan and then at the child, where her gaze lingered. "Get him up," she said gruffly. "Be careful, Alfred."

Alfred was in the act of dismounting when a

hundred yards away the sorrel horse nickered. When he was on the ground turning toward the sleeping man and child, Joe was reaching with his left hand to slowly tip his hat away from his eyes. His right hand came out of the grass with a six-gun in it.

Alfred stood like stone gazing at the gun. The hard-faced woman sucked in a sudden breath, then glared as she said, "Put that gun down!"

Bryan continued to lie there watching them both. The woman's expression was hostile; the lanky man's expression was also hostile, but in a somewhat detached way. He said nothing.

Joe sat up very slowly, shot a quick look at the sleeping child, then back to the horseman, and accompanied a little businesslike gesture with an order. "Drop it!"

The woman's eyes narrowed. "*You* drop it. You're on private range and we don't allow trespassing. Get onto your feet and toss that gun down."

Joe did not take his eyes off the wooden-faced rangeman. Ignoring the fierce woman, he repeated his command, "Drop the gun, mister. . . . I don't have a lot of patience."

The lanky cowboy looked in the direction of the buggy, but the woman was glaring at

Joe Bryan so her cowboy let his holstered Colt fall in the grass. As soon as he had done that, Joe put up his own weapon and stood. Now he ignored the rangerider to address the woman. "Lady, I'm just tryin' to get over to Springville. I'm new to the country. The only directions I got on how to find the place was to ride southeasterly from the mountains. I wouldn't have come across your land if I'd known any other way to get down there."

Her dark gray eyes were fixed on Bryan with the intensity of a snake. As though he had offered an explanation that was almost an apology for trespassing, she said, "You saddle up, take your bastard child and don't you stop again until you're in Springville."

Joe considered the woman with rising dislike. He said, "All right, lady." He glanced briefly at the sleeping child then back to her face. "It's not a bastard child and it don't belong to me, but if it did and you were a man, I'd haul you out of that rig and dunk your head in the creek."

The woman's face reddened under her tan, and her wide mouth drew flat out in a straight and uncomprising line. "I ought to shoot you," she snapped.

Joe looked at the graying, lanky man. "You work for her, mister?"

The cowboy nodded, did not speak and did not take his eyes off Joe Bryan. While making a slow appraisal of the rangerider Joe gently wagged his head. "It must be a real bed of roses," he told the other man, and got back another of those faintly detached looks.

The woman yanked her buggy whip from its socket. "Get," she exclaimed. "Move! Wake that child and get your horse!"

Joe shifted stance, hooked both thumbs and regarded the woman calmly and speculatively. "Is your name Campbell, by any chance?"

"You said you were new to the country. If you weren't lying, you wouldn't know anyone's name."

Joe smiled coldly into the angry woman's face. "I wasn't lying, lady. . . . What did you figure on doing with that buggy whip?"

Finally, the lanky man had completed his judgment of Bryan and spoke. "Miz Campbell, you better put that whip back in the socket."

She twisted to glare back as she said, "Why? Because you'd let a saddle tramp back you down and disarm you, Alfred?"

"No ma'am," the tall man replied quietly. "Because I don't think Mister Campbell would approve of someone maybe gettin' hurt over a passerby an' a little kid."

The woman seemed to want to turn her anger against him, but instead she faced Joe again. "Get your horse," she said. "*Now* — right now!"

Bryan did not move. He did not like the grip that woman had on her buggy whip, and he had no intention of going after the sorrel horse, leaving the defenseless child alone, so he said, "All right, lady. Just as soon as you and him ride away."

She yelled at him. "*Now* — damn you! *Right now*. Go get your horse!"

Joe continued to stand there looking at her. He had seen angry women before but this one was in a towering rage. He walked casually toward the buggy and halted with no more than four feet separating them as he held out his gloved hand. "Give me the whip, lady," he said, and before she could speak or even react, he lunged and wrenched the whip from her, then turned and struck her drowsing buggy-mare on the rump with it. The horse lunged; the woman was hurled back against the rear of the seat, and as the rig moved past, Joe tossed the whip in the back, completing his turn to face the lanky rangeman.

The woman was yelling as she struggled to control the lines and halt the mare. Alfred watched her efforts impassively but when Joe said, "Maybe you better go help her," and Alfred turned back to face Bryan, there was a hint of reluctant approval in his eyes. He turned to toe into a stirrup as he said, "You better move along, mister. Don't waste time getting off Campbell land."

Joe picked up Alfred's six-gun from the grass, methodically shucked out the loads and handed the gun to its owner butt-first. "How in hell can you stand to work for someone like that?" he asked in a bemused tone.

Alfred holstered his gun and leaned on the saddlehorn as he gazed downward, saying, "I don't work for her. I work for Mister Campbell."

Because Joe recalled something Hawk had mentioned about a man named Campbell, he said, "I heard he was a miserable cuss too."

Alfred smiled a little. "Naw; he's got his rules, that's all. But he's good to work for an' pays better'n most." Alfred lifted his rein hand. "Take my advice, cowboy — don't waste any time. . . . That's not your kid?"

"No."

"Then what in tarnation are you doin' in the middle of nowhere with it?"

Joe considered the rangeman's face. "It's a long story and you likely wouldn't believe it. Besides, like you said, I better not waste time gettin' away from here. How far is it to Springville?"

Alfred pointed with an upraised arm and said, "Maybe five, six miles." Then the screams of the woman a long mile ahead made Alfred break away in a flat-out run to overtake and stop the buggy.

Joe stood watching. Alfred did not get alongside the rig for another mile, and by the time he got the frightened buggy-mare slowed, the distance was too great for the distraught woman's furious vituperation to reach Joe. But he had an idea what some of the words might be.

He got the sorrel, brought him in to be rigged out, and as he had done before, had everything ready before awakening the little boy.

This time the child tanked up at the creek. And he was hungry again. Jerky did not dispel hunger, it temporarily alleviated it, and it was all Joe had. He gave the child another stick, hauled him up behind the cantle and set a corrected course in the direction the Campbell rider had indicated.

The heat was leaving; so was direct sunlight. During the altercation back at the creek the sun had gone down behind distant mountain ranges in the west without anyone noticing.

The child shifted his grip from the back of Joe's shirt to his shellbelt. He did not make a sound as he gnawed jerky.

Joe reaffirmed his earlier observation; unless future meetings and events were drastically different from everything that had happened to him since reaching New Mexico, his visit down here was going to set some kind of record for brevity. So far he had met one crazy old squawman, a venomous woman, and had riding behind his cantle a child he knew practically nothing about and who clung to him like a cub bear does to its mother. And that was another unfriendly encounter he'd had — that old fighting sow bear back up on the big meadow.

He thought he saw rooftops and trees but dusk was settling so he could not be certain. Later, though, he saw little orange squares of light where lamps glowed from behind windows.

Closer still, he picked up the aroma of cooking. So, evidently, did the child because he became restless, making those little puppy-sounds again. Joe said, "All right. You just hang on a little longer and we'll find a place to eat."

The child's restlessness did not abate, however. By the time Joe found an alley and turned down it seeking a livery barn, he had an uneasy feeling that hunger was not the only reason for the writhing and squirming behind his cantle.

He dismounted in the alley but left the child up there as he led Red into a poorly lighted livery barn runway where the customary aroma of meadow hay and ammonia from wet horse stalls was stronger than usual, indicating that whoever operated this business did not follow the usual rule of liverymen about keeping stalls dunged out and dry.

At the sound of a horse being led inside, the hostler appeared out of a dingy little harness room. He was as thin as a stick, shriveled and wiry. He also smelled slightly of old popskull when he got close enough for Joe to catch a scent of his breath. That seemed to be something else that went with being liverymen and hostlers.

The rumpled old man watched Joe lift the child down, eyed them both, and privately deciding there was absolutely no resemblance, blandly said, "Fine lookin' little girl you got, mister."

Joe nodded impassively. "Little boy . . . Stall, bait of grain, a good cuffing-down and plenty of hay. And don't put him in a stall with a soggy floor. He's never had thrush and I'd as soon he never got it."

Joe handed over a silver dollar. The old man's annoyance at that remark about dirty stalls died before it could blossom. A silver cartwheel was a lot of money to someone whose monthly wage was six dollars, not enough for whiskey and food both, which probably had something to do with the old man's emaciated appearance.

"Café still open?" Joe asked.

The old man was stuffing the coin into a ragged pocket in filthy old ill-fitting trousers as he replied, "Yes, sir. Go right on up out'n here an' you'll be on Main Street. Across the road is a glass winder with 'Café' wrote on it in black. It'll be open for another couple hours, but mostly by now everyone's ate supper. . . . Don't worry about the sorrel horse."

Joe nodded. "I won't. Thanks." He held his hand down for the child to cling to it, and started up toward the roadway through shadows moving from a smoking overhead coal-oil lantern.

What little could be seen of Springville at night when there was no moon was encouraging. Large old trees lined both sides of the roadway. Wooden plankwalks ran between the trees and storefronts, most of which were dark now. A few buildings, such as the Springville Savings Bank and the combination jailhouse and marshal's office, were of red brick. A few, but not many, buildings were much older. They had log walls dating back to frontier times when Springville had been named differently and its inhabitants had survived by developing the knack of sleeping with one eye open.

The café was between two much larger establishments, the savings bank and the mercantile store. The overweight caféman was nearly bald and had a droopy dragoon-style mustache. When Joe entered, the caféman was washing down his counter and looked up through his thick eyeglasses without a welcoming smile. He nodded when Bryan did, shifted his attention to the child, and said, "Well now, young lady — I just happen to have some fresh berry pie an' milk. How does that sound?"

Joe boosted the child onto the counter bench and answered the caféman with the same mildly pained expression he had used toward the hostler. "He's a boy, not a girl, an' if you got it we'd both like some good hot beef and potatoes."

The caféman straightened up. He seemed

to have made the same comparison the hostler had, and found no likeness between the dark child and the fair-haired, husky man. He nodded and walked away. As soon as the child was settled, holding to the edge of the counter with both hands, Joe looked around for something to put under him because only his eyes reached to the countertop. He found three mail order catalogs which gave the precise elevation the child needed. After that, the child's dark eyes roamed around the room and came to rest on the pie table with glass bowls over its three cakes and two pies.

When the caféman returned with one large supper plate and one small one, he put a small child's fork on the child's plate, then beamed. "Knew someday I'd have use for that," he told Joe. "Raised three myself. All gone now, scattered from Missouri up to Montana. . . . How old is he?"

Joe was cutting the child's food as he replied. "I don't exactly know."

The caféman's pale eyes behind thick glasses widened. Joe went right on making small pieces of meat and potatoes on the child's plate. "By any chance do you know some folks in Springville named Turner?"

The caféman did. "Wes an' Mary Jane Turner?"

Joe was trying to get the child to use the fork instead of his hands as he replied, "Yep. Those are the ones. You happen to know where they live?"

This time the answer was delayed so long that Joe abandoned his effort with the fork and left the child to eat with his fingers. He looked at the caféman. "Something wrong?"

The caféman cleared his throat. "Friends of yours, mister?"

"Mary Jane Turner is my sister."

"I see. . . . Well — Wes died last winter."

Joe gazed at the caféman without moving for a long time. So long in fact that the caféman said, "You knew Wes had lung fever? For a spell it didn't seem to be gettin' worse, then last winter we had lots of snow an' rain and wet weather, and the last time I saw him walkin' out front he looked real bad."

Joe was over his initial shock. "His wife . . . ?"

"Still lives in the white house just south of the church. Lots of flowers out front. Only house on Main Street that's got flowers all along the front of it." The caféman's eyes strayed from Bryan back to the child. He not only ate with his fingers but he had food all over his lower face and more down the front of his dirty red shirt. The caféman rolled his eyes as he said, "I'll fetch a towel."

CHAPTER 5

Springville

Mary Jane came to the door in a loose wrapper and slippers. She had a strong face with the kind of complexion that was usually found on women fifteen years younger. She was, in fact, a handsome woman whose silvery curls added a particular distinction.

She smiled and started to reach for her brother, then stopped and looked down. The child was staring upward at her. She stared back for a moment, her smile diminishing as she raised her eyes to Joe's face and without a word stepped aside for him to enter.

As she closed the door she looked at the little boy again, and said, "Joe . . . ?"

He dumped his hat beside a chair on the floor. "Nice to see you too, Mary. It's been awhile. I heard about Wes at the café. I'm sorry."

She drew the wrapper closer and pointed to a chair. "I'll get some coffee. . . . Joe, it's wonderful to see you. . . . I'm sorry; I just didn't expect — the little girl."

He eyed her thoughtfully, then looked down at the child standing so close to his leg he could feel its warmth. "Tell me something, Mary. Why does everyone think it's a little girl?"

"Isn't it? The long wavy hair, and it's so small."

"It is a little boy," Joe stated, still looking at the child. "Tomorrow if you got some shears I'm goin' to cut his hair."

"Joe . . . ?"

He sighed. "Let's go to the kitchen for that coffee, an' if you got something to lace it with, I'll tell you about him."

Her cornflower-blue eyes lingered on Joe's face. "He looks — part Indian."

"He is. His mother was half an' I think his father was all white."

She continued to stare. "He's not yours?"

Joe smiled without a shred of humor. "Can you put some body into the coffee?"

She led the way to the kitchen. It was spotless, which made Joe more conscious of the child's filthiness and his own unshaven appearance. He put the child on a chair. It promptly crawled down and went over beside the stove and curled up on the floor. Joe reddened, looked apologetically at his sister and went to lift the child. "If you got a bed, Mary . . . He's about worn out."

She took him to a small room, also immaculate, with an iron bed in one corner. He put the child down, covered it, straightened up and left his sister in the doorway staring at the sleeping child.

At the kitchen table he slumped in a chair watching his sister brewing a pot of fresh coffee. Several times she cast a sideline glance in his direction which he pretended not to notice. When she was pouring whiskey into his coffee cup, though, he watched her closely.

She did not appear to have changed much since he had last seen her. She was perhaps slightly more sturdy-looking, and her hair was silver now, but otherwise she looked exactly as she had the last time they had been together.

When she brought the coffee and sat down he began his recitation, and because it all seemed part of a whole he also included the episode of the old sow bear.

She listened, sipped coffee and studied him. When he held out his cup for a refill she returned to the stove. As she was tipping in more whiskey she said, "Why would he do that? Why would anyone abandon a little child?"

Joe had no answer beyond some uncharitable speculations he had considered since awakening in the predawn to the sound of the little boy howling. "I can't tell you, but I'm as sure he planned that as I am that I'm sitting here. What I can't figure out is why the old devil stole the child in the first place."

"Did he say anything about the father?"

"Only that he was a trader. No name, not even any towns he might travel through."

"Joe — maybe the father is dead too."

He held the cup up gazing at it. This idea had not occurred to him, but for some reason he could not define, he did not believe the child's father was dead. He shrugged. "Maybe . . . What do I do with him?"

"Does he know his name?"

"He can't talk, Mary."

She stared. "How old is he?"

Joe gazed at her. "I got no idea. I just told you all I know."

She said, "He's at least four years old, Joe. He certainly should be able to talk."

Joe sipped the hot coffee until a heart-sinking thought struck him. Three times in his life he'd encountered rangemen who were mutes. He put the cup aside and stared at the tabletop. "Maybe he can't talk, Mary." He rose and walked toward the alley door, stopped and turned back looking at her. "I had some notion you might mind him for a while. I got to find work an' no one's going to hire a rider with a little child tagging along with him. . . . But now there's something else: If he's a mute, who'd want to take him in?"

She returned her brother's look but without the troubled expression. "Come over here and sit down." He obeyed. "More laced coffee, Joe?"

"No thanks. I can feel those two cups all the way to my toes an' we just ate supper."

She nodded brusquely, already thinking beyond tonight at the kitchen table. "First thing in the morning if you'll fetch in water from the well, I'll heat it on the stove and we'll give him a bath. He's — he smells, Joe."

He nodded about that. It had been less noticeable outside but still noticeable.

"Then he needs some new clothes — a shirt and trousers. . . . Doesn't he have any shoes?"

"If he does I never saw them. He was barefoot when I first unwrapped him from that old blanket."

"You'll have to buy them, Joe. I'm barely getting by on what Wes left."

"I'll get them, an' anything else you need. Make out a list in the morning. I got some savings in my moneybelt here." Tapping his waist, he gazed fondly at her. "Y'know, you always were my favorite human being. . . . The caféman said it was lung fever that took Wes off."

She nodded. "He'd had it for years. He would be fine during the summer. Wintertime he suffered. Last winter was bad for wetness and cold. I kept him beside the stove as much as I could. Joe, it's a terrible thing to say, but when you watch someone you love dying by inches you pray for the Good Lord to take him — quickly, in his sleep."

Bryan nodded glumly. He had known Wes before he had married Mary Jane. They had been good friends. He said no more on this subject. He mused to himself that since arriving in New Mexico he had been nearly overwhelmed with one unpleasant thing after another. About his dead brother-in-law, he'd had no inkling at all.

She pulled his thoughts back to the present. "Town Marshal Henry Glover might be able to find the child's father. I would imagine the father must be frantic. . . . The old man named Hawk — was he crazy?"

Joe looked at his sister from slightly narrowed eyes. "Crazy enough to get me into this mess by plannin' how he'd do it, right down to not bein' anywhere around when I woke up with that little kid bundled about thirty feet from my bedroll. . . . I'd give a month's pay to get my hands on that sly-faced little shriveled-up weasel."

"Could you track him in the mountains, Joe?"

"Mary, a posse of full-grown Indian trackers couldn't run him down in those mountains. He told me how he'd watched soldiers and their scouts go right past where he was hiding. But even if I found him — what good would that do?"

"He could tell you the child's name and where his father is."

Joe reached for the cup, but it was empty so he shoved it away. "I got a hunch a man couldn't even beat those things out of Hawk. . . . We got to expect he's never going to show up, an' plan from there. Do you know any folks in Springville who'd take in a little boy — after his hair's cut and he's washed all over and dressed in decent clothes?"

She glanced toward the stove, went after another cup of coffee for herself, and did not reply until she was back again at the table. "He's a halfbreed, Joe."

It was less what she had said than the tone she had said it in that made his jaw muscles ripple. Of course she was right; people did not take in 'breed waifs. "There's got to be a place somewhere, Mary."

She finished her coffee and glanced at the wind-up clock on the wall. "I'll show you a bedroom; come along. Does he wake up in the night?"

"I guess he does. He's got a powerful set of lungs. When something upsets him you can hear him all the way to . . . Mary, he can't be a mute if he can yell like that, can he?"

She led him back through the parlor and to a door in the south wall. It was cold in there because she only heated the rooms she lived in, which were a bedroom, the kitchen and the parlor.

She left him with a small lamp and went back to the kitchen to wash their cups and put away the bottle of whiskey. Then she stood in the doorway of the small, dark room where the little boy was sleeping.

He was making panting sounds as he slept so she got a towel to wipe his face. It was too hot in the little room. She went back to the kitchen to close down the stove damper than returned to the bedside, made certain the child was well covered, and stopped again in the doorway looking at the bed.

Eventually she went to her own bedroom to lie awake in the darkness, the same thing her brother was doing on the opposite side of the house.

She couldn't be blamed for her initial reaction to see her brother arrive with a part-Indian child. Such things were by no means rare, even now when most of the Indians had been corralled on reservations.

Joe's thoughts in the darkness of his bedroom paralleled his sister's. He too had seen dozens of examples of the very thing she had first thought. Nor did he feel particularly isolated from the brotherhood of rangemen because of the idea. What troubled him was that in this case it was not true, he was not the father. More troubling was the hunch that he would be unable to get clear of the responsibility old Hawk had saddled him with. And if the little boy could not talk, or had a speech difficulty of some kind, whatever chance might otherwise exist of finding him a home would vanish.

He slept finally, but not very well. In the morning his sister was already boiling water in a big tub atop the stove when he got out to the kitchen. She had a cloth tightly wound around her head, her face was flushed, and when he protested that she should have waited for him to fetch in water from the well, she pointed to the table where someone had left very little of a large meal. "I don't see how he can be so small and eat so much. . . . Sit down, I'll get you something."

"No. No, you won't. I'll eat down at the café. Where is he?"

She jerked her head sideways. "In his bedroom taking off those filthy clothes. Hurry back, Joe. It would be embarrassing if some of my women friends came by and he was running around the house naked."

That did not seem to be much of a problem to Joe. "When you've scrubbed him you could put him in the same clothes until I get back."

"He has lice, Joe."

He looked at his sister. Despite the perspiration, the overheated kitchen, the work she'd already gone to, she had a sparkle in her eye and purpose in her motions. As he went after his hat before leaving the house he told himself that she *liked* this.

He did not dwell upon how this could be; but even if he had, there was no possibility that he would have come up with such things as the heart-stunning loneliness of widowhood or the compounded sensation of widowhood and childlessness, which together fed a feeling of futility and failure in a robust, handsome woman of forty-five who had desired a family above everything else, and who had been denied one through reasons she did not understand.

Outside, Springville looked much better than it had last night. There was light horse-back and wheeled traffic in the broad road-way, people along both plankwalks, sunlight bouncing off glass windows, and when he crossed over to walk southward in the direc-tion of the café and saw the tonsorial parlor with its proprietor sitting on his barber chair smoking a cigar and looking bored, he walked in. Breakfast could wait.

The barber arose, snuffed out his stogie and flourished a large apron to cover Joe from gullet to knees as he opened their associa-tion with the customary comments on the weather. Joe said very little; there was no need for him to. The barber was a born con-versationalist who rarely paused for another opinion.

Joe paid his two bits for a shave and shear-ing. Then he went down to the café smelling strongly of French toilet water. He and the caféman exchanged a nod. As Joe sat down between two lean, leathery rangeriders, each one turned slowly and inhaled his fragrance, winked behind his back at one another then went back to their breakfasts.

The caféman brought a morning steak with

fried potatoes, limp toast, and black java. He looked around with exaggerated interest, then leaned to ask where the little boy was. Joe chewed and swallowed before answering.

"Getting a bath." He went back to his meal in an attitude that plainly implied he did not care about pursuing this subject. The café-man walked up his counter to collect silver coins from a large, heavy-boned graying man with a dull and dented badge on his shirt-front.

The caféman shot a darting look at Joe, who was too busy eating to notice. The café-man then leaned and whispered to the big-boned, craggy-face man, turned and went behind a curtain to his cooking area while the big man with the badge sucked his teeth, picked up a toothpick, and using that as a reason to continue to stand looking around the room, made a close study of Joe Bryan before eventually departing.

One of the lean rangemen sitting beside Joe nudged him gently and said, "Maybe you'd want to know, mister: The town marshal was sure studyin' you up, down an' crossways."

The cowboys left. Joe finished his breakfast and stood up. When the caféman arrived to collect his coins Joe looked steadily at him, long enough to make him fidget. Then Joe walked out into the overhang shade, heading for the mercantile emporium. He did not see the big-boned town marshal watching him from across the roadway in a recessed doorway.

CHAPTER 6

Making Acquaintances

The paunchy individual wearing black sleeve-protectors from the wrist to the elbow of his striped shirt told Joe that buying clothing for a child whose size he did not know was not any great difficulty, providing the buyer could indicate the child's height. Joe held his hand palm down beside his leg where the child had leaned against him last night. The store clerk nodded and went briskly to work selecting underwear, pants and two shirts.

He balked when Joe mentioned boots. That, he said, was something different. With pants you could roll up the cuffs and with shirts you could roll up the sleeves. There was considerable leeway, but with leather boots . . . He wagged his head. "Mister, if this stuff is maybe a birthday present or something, we might come fairly close, but leather just don't give much nor shrink at all." He eyed Joe's exasperated expression. "How far does the child live? Is there a chance he would be comin' to Springville soon?"

Joe ignored the question while eyeing several pair of children's boots. The pair with copper toe-guards looked about right, so he pointed to them. "Put 'em in the box. If they don't fit I'll come back and swap 'em for a pair that do."

The clerk obeyed, totaled the purchases and handed Joe the slip of paper. Joe said nothing; he paid up and walked out with his bundles. He stopped on the plankwalk: for what it had cost him to rig the little boy out fresh he could have bought a new saddleblanket, or spent a week in a hotel somewhere sleeping up off the ground.

He added this to his grudge against Hawk.

The pair of rangemen who had sat on each side of him at the café were standing at the tierack in front of the pool hall idly watching Joe striding toward them. One of them grinned slyly and said, "Here comes Rosebud from the café." The other man hitched his shellbelt as he straightened off the rail. "I expect he'll have some nice nighties and whatnot in them packages. Maybe with lace frillies on 'em."

Joe saw the men; they looked familiar, but he continued to walk until he was a couple hundred feet south, then stepped down into the roadway to cross over.

One of the cowboys strolled back near the rear of his horse and softly said, "Hey, sweet-pea."

Joe turned. It only occurred to him that the cowboy was addressing him when he saw the man's indolent, teasing smile and direct stare.

"Hey, sweetpea, what's in them bundles — pink longjohns maybe, or frilly underpants?"

Joe gazed at them. He was puzzled but he was also knowledgeable about taunts of this kind. He shifted his grip on the packages and turned fully back toward them. "Something eating you?" he asked the rider who was doing the talking.

His friend spoke up. "Naw, except that we don't like grown men dressin' like rangemen who wear perfume."

Joe turned his attention to this man. "Perfume?"

"Sure. You smelled like perfume in the café. We had to set on both sides of you."

Joe began to suspect what this was about. He eyed them both. They were younger than he was; neither one of them weighed within thirty pounds of what he weighed, and they were either bullies or ignorant. He suspected it might be a mixture of both.

"Well now," he said slowly, walking back

to the edge of the plankwalk, "I spent an hour gettin' shaved and shorn, and the gent who runs the tonsorial shop sprinkled some of that perfumed water on me. . . . You boys never been in a tonsorial shop where they did that?"

The man closest to Joe Bryan was no longer smiling. He looked uncomfortable. With very little distance separating them he could not avoid comparisons. Joe Bryan was powerfully put together. The other rider, still standing near the rear of his horse, sauntered forward, only half-smiling now, the other half of his expression mean.

"Where we come from, grown men don't allow no barber to sprinkle that stinkin' stuff on 'em. Only sissies and kind of strange men allow it."

Joe switched his attention to this man and leaned to put his packages on the edge of the duckboards. The pair of rangemen looked quickly at one another. The sneering man took a fast step forward and aimed a kick as Joe was beginning to straighten up.

Behind the rangemen but within Joe's range of sight because he was facing in that direction, a very large, thick man suddenly roared and charged forward. The cowboys, concentrating on Joe Bryan, were startled and unprepared. The big man did not give them a chance to get set. He hit the nearest man in the soft parts, dropping him into the manured dust of the roadway writhing and gagging, and stepped past heading for the second man. That was the disagreeable cowboy, except that now his face had been wiped clear of any expression. He was half turned, twisted from the waist, when the town marshal caught his arm and wrenched him fully around. Joe knew what was going to happen and winced in advance. The big town marshal hit that one up alongside the head. The cowboy was knocked backward and fell like a sack of wet grain. He was on his stomach, and did not move at all.

Joe and the town marshal eyed each other. Joe wagged his head wryly. "Did you drop from the sky?"

The large man was working his knuckles. "I was comin' down from the stoveworks. I saw you but couldn't see them until I got past the horses at the rack. . . . You know them?"

"No. They said they were at the café when I had breakfast in there a while back."

"What was they on the peck about?"

"The barber sprinkled me with some of that rose water or whatever it is he uses. They didn't like a grown man smelling like lilacs or whatever."

Initially even the people who had passed by during the verbal exchange had paid no attention, but now there were onlookers along both plankwalks standing discreetly distant as the heavy-boned man bent over the writhing cowboy and plundered his pockets. He put the contents into the man's hat then stepped over him and did the same with the unconscious man. As he straightened he jerked his head at Joe. "Grab that crybaby by the collar and drag him along. I'll take this one."

Joe had not felt any particular rancor right from the start. He felt none now. In fact he pitied the man who had been hit so hard in the stomach he was being sick in the dirt.

The big lawman scowled, then attributed Joe's hesitation to something else and called to a man standing in a doorway. "Sam — mind this gent's packages until he gets back to pick them up." Marshal Glover then gestured. "All right, mister, the harnessmaker'll keep watch over your bundles."

Joe looked around as Sam came gravely over to get the packages. Then he shrugged, grabbed the injured man and hoisted him to his feet, gripped him around the middle and began following the marshal, who was dragging the unconscious cowboy. His boots left twin tracks in roadway dust. Onlookers neither moved nor made a sound. They seemed to have great respect for their town marshal.

Joe was embarrassed by the looks he was getting from those motionless onlookers. They appeared to be equating him somehow with the defeat of two rough-looking range-riders, but he had not raised a fist.

At the jailhouse the town marshal dragged the unconscious man down into one of the cells, left him lying face up on the floor and went after a bucket of water which he up-ended over him. It had an effect. The soaked man gasped, flailed with both arms and rolled clumsily onto his side as he coughed.

Marshal Glover returned to the office where Joe Bryan had eased the injured cow-boy down onto a wall bench. The rider wilted forward looking ill and gray, soiled down his shirtfront and in pain.

Glover went to a big, untidy old oaken table, sat down, put his hat atop the disar-rayed papers, then leaned forward with clasped hands eyeing the cowboy. "Who are you?" he growled. "Where you from?"

The cowboy continued to lean far over as he mumbled a reply. "Name's Jack Hudson."

"What's your partner's name?"

"Jim Kinkaid."

"Where you from?"

"Texas . . . only that was before we got work up here at one of the outlying' outfits."

"What outfit?"

"Campbell . . . "

Joe had been studying the seemingly heartless, big rough man at the desk. Now, he put his attention upon the gray-faced rangeman. The marshal also considered the cowboy. He asked no more questions, he arose and upended two hats and pawed through the belongings of his prisoners, and afterward indiscriminately swept things back into the hats and put them aside as he looked at Joe. "How about you, mister?"

"Name is Joe Bryan. I rode in last night from up north."

"Lookin' for work, are you?"

"Not exactly. My sister lives in Springville. She asked me to visit so I came down here."

"What's her name?"

"Mary Jane Turner."

The large man's craggy, granite-jawed face loosened. He sank down again at the table. "Wes's wife," he murmured, and gave his big head a faint shake. "You knew about Wes?"

"No. Not until I was eating supper last night over at the café and the gent who runs the place told me. Did you know him, marshal?"

Henry Glover sat back in his chair. "Knew him real well. There aren't too many around like Wes Turner. . . . The preacher was down in Santa Fé when he died. I'm the one who read from the Bible over Wes's grave. . . . Did you know him very well — what did you say your name was?"

"Joe Bryan. Yes, I knew Wes before he married my sister. I agree with what you said about him. A man don't run across very many Wes Turners."

An interlude of silence ensued, broken finally when the injured cowboy straightened up gingerly. He still looked like someone who had been kicked in the stomach by a mule, but he was evidently feeling less pain now. He said, "Marshal, we was just fixin' to have a little fun. Maybe chouse him a little."

Glover's bold dark eyes bored into the man. Joe's earlier suspicion that Henry Glover was a merciless man was reinforced by that look. "Not in this town," Glover said coldly. "Two to one — you boys like odds like that when you hunt trouble, do you? What is your . . . Hudson, wasn't it? Hudson, you don't look real good. You just set there an' recover, an' when your partner comes 'round I'm not goin' to jug you boys. You can get on back to work. Just be damned sure you remember — in this town you feel like bullyin' someone, come look me up." Glover's wide mouth split into a humorless grin. "Rough-tough rangeriders. Hell! I eat sons-of-bitches like you an' him for breakfast. You understand?"

Jack Hudson did not respond until the marshal went down into his cell to see if the man he had soaked to the skin with cold water had revived. Then Hudson said, "Feller at the ranch . . . Al Conley the tophand . . . he said to watch out for Marshal Glover."

Joe thought it had been good advice.

Hudson turned his head. "Where'd he come from?"

"Up the road behind you fellers. You were too busy figuring how to jump me to hear him until he was on top of you. . . . How are your guts?"

Hudson leaned against the wall before answering. "That old man can hit," he said softly, almost reverently. Joe thoughtfully rubbed the tip of his nose; he and Marshal Glover were about the same age. Hudson, the Campbell rider, must be very young to make a statement like that. Joe said, "This tophand — is he tall, rangy-built feller who rides a hand-carved slick-fork Texas saddle?"

Hudson's eyes were half closed. He nodded his head. "Yeah. Easy to work around."

"Who is the rangeboss?"

"He was a feller name Curtis. But he quit last month."

"Couldn't get along with Mister Campbell?"

"No. Mister Campbell's rougher'n a cob but he's not hard to work for — if you don't ride off somewhere and set in the shade when you're supposed to be working. It was that damned woman."

"Missus Campbell?"

"Yes. She's a real ringtailed roarer. Mean, cranky, wants to run everything. Her and Curtis locked horns and he upped and quit."

Joe settled more comfortably on the bench, his attention diverted from something that tickled him now but had not been funny yesterday morning when he'd encountered that woman. Marshal Glover's bull bass was bellowing from the cell. One hand gripped around Kinkaid's waist, Glover was swearing at the man he had knocked senseless, telling him to stop stumbling as they worked their way up into the office.

When they entered the office Glover shoved Jim Kinkaid toward the bench. He staggered, then fell beside Hudson. Squaring up on the bench, he drifted an aimless gaze around the room. Joe thought he looked worse off than Hudson. He was soaked from head to toe, his hair was plastered over a bluish lump where a ham-sized fist had landed. His clothing clung to his lean frame and when his gaze settled upon the heavy man over at the table, Kinkaid blew out a soggy big sigh of breath.

Glover sat glowering for a while before he said, "Go get your horses and get out of Springville and don't neither of you even think about comin' back until you're ready to mind your manners. *Get!*"

They shoved upright and went out the jail-house door as unsteady as a pair of drunks. Joe turned back from watching them and saw Henry Glover's rough smile. He too rose. Glover stopped him from departing with a question. "Is that your little boy who was over at the café with you last night?"

Joe considered his reply because he knew this was going to come up often and he'd like to have a ready answer. "I'm not his paw, but I'm lookin' out for him."

Glover seemed poised to explore this subject but Joe went to the door, and in the end Glover simply said, "You think you could have cleaned their plows — the two of them against you?"

Joe grinned. "I don't know. I only know

that while they were getting supper I'd be gettin' a little snack too."

Glover laughed and watched Bryan close the office door after himself.

CHAPTER 7

Settling In

Joe had been gone two hours doing a chore Mary Jane thought should not have taken more than a half hour. She watched him put the bundles on the table where she was resting with a cup of coffee, looking rumpled, red-faced, but satisfied about something.

He did not tell her what had happened and she did not ask. Instead she picked up the garments to examine each one closely. The small boots with their shiny copper toe-guards she examined longest, and smiled up at her brother. "It will be a miracle if they fit, Joe."

He nodded. "Where's the lad?"

"Sleeping . . . Do you like the name Wesley?"

He looked at her with an uneasy feeling. He did not believe she should get too attached to the little boy. Naming him for her dead husband was a pretty good indication that this was exactly what was happening. But he smiled at her and said, "Sure. I always did like that name."

She eyed him askance and became defensive. "Joe, we can't call him 'little boy.' "

She faced him and searched his expression for amusement, irony, something she did not find. Joe Bryan had learned many years ago to control expressions. He said, "Wesley sure sleeps a lot, don't he?"

She glanced in the direction of the door ajar off the kitchen where she had bedded him down last night. "Yes, he does. But growing children need lots of rest and good food and all, Joe."

This time he did grin at her. She reddened and arose to get him a cup of coffee from the stove, and while her back was to him she said, "A woman don't have to be a mother to know certain things, Joe." She stood with his cup in her hand, still facing away as she said something else. "Wes never knew this. No one knew this, Joe." She turned toward him slowly. "I have four books on raising children hidden in the attic. I know what they say by heart."

She brought his cup to the table and sat down without looking at him. He watched her profile, and for the first time in his forty years felt a terrible heartache for someone. He sipped coffee and said nothing — until a sudden, very unsettling thought occurred to him. *Mary Jane wanted this child.* In one day she had become what she had longed to be all her life and had never been able to be — a mother.

Oh damn, he said to himself.

She abruptly faced him with a look of triumph that scattered his thoughts like leaves.

"He can talk."

The statement completed the scattering, but he simply sat staring at her. Eventually he ventured a question. "Are you sure? What did he say?"

Her pink cheeks got pinker. "He said — 'Damn, that water's hot.' "

Joe threw back his head and roared. His sister sat smiling with very bright eyes. Noises beyond the ajar door indicated that Joe's laughter had awakened the child. Mary Jane jumped up and went to get him. He let her lead him into the kitchen where he stopped dead-still staring at the boots with the copper toe-caps. Joe leaned forward as he said, "Come over here, Wes. Don't get your hopes up; most likely they won't fit. . . . No, you got to put the socks on first. You'd really ought to have your britches on first too . . . here. Hold still will you? Those darned boots aren't goin' to fly away."

He had never dressed a child before but it

was nothing that could not be mastered the first time, except that the little boy did not want to turn his back on the boots until Joe growled; then he did.

Mary Jane was down on her knees tucking in shirttails and belting the trousers. The child had no hips. She cinched up the belt until Joe frowned and loosened it. She said the trousers would not stay up and Joe shrugged about that as he picked up one of the boots. To their surprise the child dropped down on the floor and, without help, pulled on both boots. Joe stood him up and gestured. "Walk over to the door an' back."

The child stopped directly in front of Joe, but looking down, not up at the man. Joe watched his sister feel for toes under the leather. She also pinched and squeezed on the sides of the boots. Joe and the little boy were expressionless as they awaited her judgment. She finally sat back looking puzzled. "They are a perfect fit. I don't see how you could guess that close."

He winked at the child. "I didn't, Mary. When we were kids I always wanted a pair like that. I used to lie in bed thinkin' about someday owning a pair and polishing the copper caps until they were as bright as gold. This pair was the only ones that had caps."

He told the child to walk through the parlor and return. They sat watching until he was in the kitchen again and Mary asked him if the boots pinched his feet or hurt him anywhere. As he shook his head looking up at Mary Jane, Joe grinned. Little Wesley wanted those boots so badly he would not have risked being made to take them off even if all his ten toes were curled under inside them.

Not until the excitement of the boots and new clothing had passed did Joe notice that Mary Jane had cut the child's hair. What made him particularly notice this was a powerful scent of carbolic acid each time Wes came near him. After shearing him she had also disinfected his hair and scalp.

He caught her looking mistily at the child and slapped both legs as he shot up off the chair and said, "Come along, Wes, let's go walk down the alley. You got to break boots in. Tonight we'll rub some grease into the leather to soften it up."

Mary Jane leaned in the doorway watching them go beyond the sagging rear fence into the alleyway. As they turned northward she softly closed the door and began cleaning up her kitchen.

The morning was nearly spent. It had brought the usual heat of summer with it. In the alley, with buildings to provide square blocks of shade, Joe walked slowly with the child giving considerable thought to something he wished to establish to his personal satisfaction.

He had spoken often to the little boy on the ride down from Spirit Meadow. In fact he had conversed with him the way he normally did with the sorrel horse, and not once had the child answered or even indicated that he understood what Joe was saying.

Maybe that was because nothing Joe had said had touched upon anything of real interest to the child. Also, maybe he was silent because too many frightening things had happened to him lately.

Joe looked downward. Wes was walking through alley dust watching daylight reflect off the copper toe-caps. He stopped suddenly and sank to one knee, fished out his bandana and held it out as he said, "Want to wipe the dust off?"

The child took the bandana and sat down to rub the toe-caps. Joe smiled. The child handed back the bandana and stood up, but Joe remained down on one knee. "You like 'em, Wes?"

Two large dark eyes came over to Joe's face, followed by a smile. "I like them," the child said.

Joe stood up, stuffing the bandana into a hip pocket as he blew out a sigh of relief. *That* fear could be disposed of; Wes was not mute. One difficulty remained: Finding a home. . . .

Later, with daylight waning, he turned back with the child's sweaty palm in his hand. A large brown dog walked from between two sheds on the west side of the alley, looked steadily at them and lowered a broad, flat head as it growled. Wes's small hand convulsively gripped Joe's fingers as the child stumbled, regained his balance and pushed as close as he could to Joe's leg. He was terrified.

Joe stopped, knelt and put his arm roughly around the child's shoulders. "Just a dog," he said. "He's not going to hurt you." Wes was glassy-eyed with fear so Joe hoisted him, swung him across his shoulders and continued walking. The dog did not retreat but neither did it move out into the alley. Joe could feel the child's body quivering as they came abreast of the dog and continued on past. The dog had evidently been guarding its territory — a tarpaper shack farther off which seemed to be on the same plot of ground as the ramshackle sheds.

The dog slunk back out of sight and Joe swung Wes to the ground, but for the balance of their stroll the child watched over his shoulder, and when they were back in Mary Jane's kitchen Joe told her about the dog and said either Wes had been injured by a dog or he had a natural fear of them.

The following morning Joe used tools he found in a shed and repaired the neglected backyard fence. He even rehung the gate and made a latch for it, Wes staying with him throughout most of this. When Joe missed him and went looking, he found the child curled up in a flowerbed asleep.

Mary Jane took him inside, washed him and put him down for a nap; then she came out back to tell her brother that Wes must have learned from his parents to go off like that and sleep. Joe agreed with her, but he thought old Hawk would have allowed the child to do that too.

Joe put the tools back in the shed, told his sister she could allow the child to play in the fenced yard, then went out the front door and headed for the saloon. Hot weather and beer went together; otherwise Joe Bryan was not much of a drinker.

For a while he wanted to be alone, at least out of his sister's house. He had never been a domestic individual. He had nothing against being domesticated; he simply had never lived that way.

The saloon had a few customers, perhaps a dozen of them, but it was too early for the evening trade so the barman was willing to lean and talk to Joe when he asked about the Campbell ranch. The barman, who was short and barrel-shaped, put a pale-eyed gaze on his new customer as he said, "It's big. Old Campbell come into this country when a man still had to sleep with his back to a wall or Indians'd cut his throat and steal his horse. They tell me old James Campbell was married once, but I been here goin' onto twenty years and he ain't been married in that length of time. . . . Minds his ranch, upgrades his cattle, takes real pride in the quality of his horses, and keeps three, four riders year round. Summers, like now, he'll have as many as eight men riding for him."

Joe half drained his beer glass. "Do you know him?"

The barman deliberated before replying. "Yeah, but not real well. He's been in here a few times but I got the impression he's not much of a drinkin' man."

"You sure his wife died long ago?"

The barman was sure. "Positive. If he ever really had one."

Joe considered the sticky ring on the bartop around his beer glass. "Well, the other day I was crossin' his land an' a woman called Missus Campbell came along in a buggy, with a feller named Alfred, and she went up one side of me an' down the other."

The barman softly scowled. "What for?"

"Trespassing, she said."

The barman dug out a red bandana, thunderously blew his nose and pocketed the bandana before speaking again. "An' you bein' a stranger an' all, figured that was his wife?"

"That's about the size of it."

"Well, no sir, that's not his wife, that's his dead brother's wife. Her husband passed on in early spring and she came out here to get away from her home back in Missouri." The barman raised a thick, short arm to indicate he had heard a patron thumping the bartop for a refill, and nodded before walking away from Joe Bryan.

There was no reason to hurry through the glass of beer, so Joe leaned in comfort and sipped, and when that glass had been emptied he too thumped the bartop.

As the barman set up his second glassful he jerked his head. "That feller who wanted a refill, that's the *remudero* for Campbell. His name is Gonsalvo Acosta. They call him Gus. Him and the old man been together a lot of years. Difference is that Gus ain't wearin' out and old Campbell is."

"How many cattle does he run?" Joe asked, and the barman rolled up his eyes and spread his palms. "More'n anyone else in the countryside. I can only guess. I'd say maybe three, four thousand cows, and a bull to every forty cows. I'm not good at sums. You can add it up. It's a lot of cattle any way you look at it."

Joe nodded in agreement. "Lot of cattle," he murmured, then asked another question. "They tell me he pays good and isn't too hard to ride for."

The barman did not look at Joe as he replied; he was looking at the *remudero*. "There's some say he's impossible and then again there's those as say as long as a man does his work, Mister Campbell's good to work for. As for pay, I don't know." Now, finally, the barman looked around. "You interested in goin' to work for him?"

Joe finished off his second glass of beer, placed some silver coins atop the bar and smiled. "I'm interested in goin' to work for someone. I need some spending money."

The barman was sympathetic. He too had once ridden for a living. His private opinion, never voiced in the saloon, was that any man with the sense God gave a goose would find another line of work. But what he said to Joe did not even hint of this.

"I know for a fact," the barman said, "they're down a man. The foreman quit a week or so back. That means the tophand'll be runnin' things, and *that* means someone else has got to move up an' do the tophand's job. What can you lose, mister? Ride out and talk to Al Conley, he's the tophand doin' the foreman's job now."

Joe's face showed nothing. He thanked the barman and returned to the roadway and its fading daylight. He had already talked to Alfred Conley, the rangerider that disagreeable woman had tried to make fight Joe. In fact he had disarmed him, and while Conley had impressed Joe as a sensible man, it would be asking an awful lot of a man who had been disarmed and humiliated to hire the man who had done those things to him.

He wandered down to the livery barn to look in on Red. He also wanted to make sure his Winchester was still in its saddleboot.

CHAPTER 8

Campbell Riders

After breakfast the following morning Joe headed for the livery barn to saddle up and sashay over the countryside looking for work. It was not his intention to ride westward, the direction of the Campbell outfit, but — as he had been continually discovering through one calamity after another — fate here in the New Mexico Territory was not only perverse but also liable to take a very strong if invisible hand in people's lives.

He had covered no more than four miles on the stage road when he saw horsemen loping in his general direction. It was difficult to count them because they rode all in a bunch.

Red plodded up the road as though he might do so until the road ended on the horizon somewhere. The morning was blessedly warm, the sky was as clear as glass, and there was no wind.

Joe watched the riders because in his field of vision nothing else was moving. He eventually concentrated on just one man, the horseman in the lead, and the longer he watched, the more confident he was that he knew him. Alfred Conley.

The riders swung southward. They would not have touched the road for another mile but as they loped parallel to Joe the rangy man out front raised a gloved hand slightly.

Joe blew out a rough breath and said, "Red, he's sure got everything in his favor this time," and since it went against his grain to run, he sat waiting in the middle of the road.

The riders came ahead at a loose trot, setting their gait to that of Alfred Conley. When they were close enough, Joe recognized Hudson and Kinkaid, the men Glover had whipped, and one more. He was a Mexican, not very tall and a little fleshy. He was very dark. It was the man the bartender in town had identified as the Campbell outfit's *remudero,* Gonsalvo Acosta.

Conley stopped and gazed at Joe Bryan. The tophand sat relaxed atop a fine-looking liver-chestnut horse with four stocking feet. Joe nodded. Conley nodded back and broke the silence. "Good morning. You wasn't figuring on turning left over Campbell range, was you?"

Joe shook his head. "Not for a lot of money.

I got broke to lead about doing that the last time we met."

Conley had even, strong features and laugh-wrinkles around his eyes. "Where's your little boy?"

Joe debated his answer before saying, "Back in town. And he's not my little boy. I'm just lookin' out for him." He gave look for look with the Campbell tophand. "Did that lady get over being mad?"

Conley's eyes twinkled. "She still hasn't. She got a few bumps."

"I'm glad she didn't get hurt."

"She wouldn't believe that. She yelled at me all the way back to the yard that you tried to kill her."

Joe nodded. He had exhausted everything he could think of to say to Alfred Conley. Then he remembered what the barman had told him and counted the riders. Including Conley there were six, which was short at least one of what the barman had thought was Campbell's normal riding crew.

Conley cut into his thoughts. "You any good with livestock?"

Joe's reply was very short. "Average. Why?"

"You want a job?"

This time Joe squinted at the rangy man. "Workin' for you?"

"For my boss, James Campbell. We're down a rider. It seemed to me over at the creek you might be interested in goin' to work."

Joe asked what Campbell paid and Conley told him. The wage was slightly higher than was customary. "Anything special?"

Conley shook his head.

Joe lightly rubbed the tip of his nose. "Is your name Conley?"

"Yes."

"Well now, Mister Conley, if that lady saw me in your yard she'd shoot me."

Conley laughed and the other men smiled. "She drove the buggy over to Springville this morning to catch the stage. She's goin' back to Missouri. Her visit at the ranch is over. . . . What's your name?"

"Joe Bryan."

"Well, Mister Bryan, if you were about to start out hunting work, you didn't find it, it found you. Any objections?"

Joe looked among the men again, then back to the rangeboss. "You one of those folks who carry a grudge, Mister Conley?"

The tophand laughed again. "No. I wasn't too happy about Mrs. Campbell either. . . . Let's go; we got to sweep this end of our range and maybe find a band of horses that don't seem to be any other place that we've looked since yesterday. . . . And that's the last time I'm going to call you 'mister.' You ready?"

Joe was ready. He was also uneasy about all this happening so abruptly and unexpectedly, particularly since he had intended to avoid the Campbell outfit as if they were a den of rattlers. He reined off the road and joined the loose lope of the riders. He would have to get word to his sister that he wouldn't be back for a spell, but at the moment that was not topmost among his thoughts.

He was riding beside the *remudero*, who raised a gloved hand in a little salute and introduced himself. He had eyes as black as midnight. They were small and partially concealed by what appeared to be a perpetual squint. Otherwise, his features were coarse but there was warmth in his smile. Joe returned the little salute and spoke his name, which all the riders had heard before.

Acosta said, "Call me Gus. You're Joe. I think I saw you in the saloon yesterday."

Joe nodded. "Yeah. What about these horses we're lookin' for, Gus?"

The Mexican raised his shoulders and dropped them. "They was supposed to be northwest of here. Up where most of the loose stock is grazed. We only pulled their shoes an' turned 'em out last week. We'd been riding them on a gather. . . . Now you know as much as I know."

Joe eyed the *remudero*. "Tracks?"

Acosta shook his head and gestured. "Tracks everywhere. Campbell ranch runs two hunnerd head of saddle and harness stock. They're all barefoot on the range, an' they been over here as well as everyplace else. Joe, we got to see 'em, otherwise we're not going to find 'em."

Al Conley and another rawboned man were riding together up front. The other man was towheaded and tanned brown, which made his light hair seem even lighter. He and the tophand were discussing something Joe could not quite make out.

Gus Acosta leaned slightly from the saddle with a question. "What was that between you an' Al about a creek an' the woman?"

Joe stood in his stirrups looking intently ahead and to the right. "Nothing," he told the *remudero*. "That's where Conley an' I met before. Ask him. . . . Gus — skyline over yonder and southward. Is that dust?"

The Mexican raised in his stirrups too but since he was short-legged it did not give him much more elevation than he'd had sitting down. But he had the eyesight of an eagle. He also had another distinction, unique among Mexicans: Joe saw his jaws working on a cud. Mexicans almost never chewed tobacco, they smoked it. There was something else to confirm Joe's suspicion that despite looks and breeding Gus Acosta had been neither born in Mexico nor raised there: He had absolutely no accent.

Acosta abruptly called ahead to Al Conley and gestured. Everyone's attention swung in the direction of the very distant dust banner. Conley hauled back down to a walk and for a long while nothing was said. Then — something else Joe was to learn about Gus Acosta — the *remudero* showed impatience and annoyance. He glanced briefly at Joe and muttered under his breath, "What's he want, an engraved invitation? Those horses aren't drifting. This time of day horses don't move fast or far; they tank up and go stand in shade until the heat's gone. They're being driven."

When they had plodded a half mile Acosta suddenly called ahead again. "I'll take the new man an' go scout. All right, Al?"

Conley twisted from the waist, eyed Joe and shrugged. "Go ahead, just be real careful. They're probably runnin' scairt from something — wolf, pack of coyotes. We'll keep watch."

Gus barely grunted at Joe. "Ride!"

When they were widening the distance from the others, Gus vigorously shook his head and swore. Then he said, "Pack of coyotes! A wolf! How can someone who's real good with livestock be so darned dumb sometimes?" To emphasize his point Gus gestured with a thick, short arm. "Those horses are being driven. Look at the dust. Scairt horses bust out in all directions. Drove horses are kept bunched up by whoever's driving them."

Joe studied the dust, which was about all either of them could see at that distance. It looked like any other cloud of dust to him until he had watched it for a long time, then he glanced at Acosta with dawning respect. He was right: Whatever was making that dust was moving straight south and was doing so in a collected way.

He raised his voice to the man ten feet to his right. "Can you see what's under the dust?"

Acosta made another of those irritable arm gestures. "Horses."

Joe knew no more than he had known before asking. He strained to make out solid objects below the dust banner but failed.

"Who would be driving them, Gus?"

The *remudero* turned his head to stare. "Thieves. It's none of us from the home place."

"In broad morning daylight?"

Gus shot another testy look at his companion, but this time checked his impulse to be brusque. "You never been in this country before?"

"No."

Gus made another wide gesture. "Lots of horses are run off in broad daylight. If thieves get a good start an' let the old mares, colts and cripples filter out an' keep the good stock running . . . Joe, it's only a two-days' run to the Mex border. If they keep 'em moving at night — after all, all they got to do is keep headin' straight south — but if anyone's after them, they got to be able to see something or the pursuers can angle off an' by morning be five miles in the wrong direction." As he finished talking, Gus raised in the stirrups again, then hauled his horse down to a walk. The heat was increasing and horses were not machines.

Gus looked dour as he fished for a plug, worried off a corner of it, and pocketed what remained. Rounding the piece of chewing tobacco by rolling it between his palms, he popped it into his mouth and tongued it up into his cheek. He asked if Joe chewed and got a negative head-wag.

Gus rode with his hatbrim low and his black eyes narrowed to slits. For a while he and Joe

Bryan'd had Springville's trees in sight off to their left, but an hour and a half later there were no landmarks that Joe recognized.

They loped again for two miles, then Gus turned off and dropped to a steady walk to cool his horse out. He went directly to a creek and swung off to loosen the cinch, slip the bit and water his animal. Joe followed. As Gus stood waiting he eyed Joe's sorrel horse. "Got bottom?" he asked. Joe nodded watching Red tank up. "Hope he does," stated Acosta. "Just once I'd like to have someone along who'll stay with me until we catch those sons-of-bitches. . . . You hate horsethieves, Joe?"

"Yeah, but I don't want this bunch bad enough to founder my horse to catch them."

Gus chewed and scanned the rearward distance until the horses were watered and rested, then as he snugged up his cinch and eased on the bridle, he said, "I don't see the others."

Joe looked across his saddleseat. It dawned on him slowly that if the Campbell crew was not in sight, and did not appear soon, he and Gus were going to be pressing the pursuit of horsethieves on into the darkness, alone.

Since horsemen never loped horses right after they had filled up on water, they walked them. Joe had started out this morning feeling normal and hopeful. All he had had in mind was finding work for some cattle outfit. He'd found it — entirely by accident, or as a result of something anyway — but instead of doing routine stock work, he was now caught up in what could become a shooting scrape, and that sure as hell had been the furthest thing from his thoughts even after he'd encountered the Campbell riding crew. Studying his companion carefully, he said, "Gus, do you know this country down here?"

Acosta nodded. "Yeah. We're still on Mister Campbell's land." He saw the look on Joe's face and laughed. "He owns more range than most folks could drive over in a week. I've been with him a long time. I've rode over every darned foot of his range one time or another. Otherwise how would I have known where that creek was we just watered at?" At Joe's lingering stare Acosta widely grinned showing perfect big white teeth. "I'm sixty-five."

Joe didn't believe it but he kept that to himself and asked another question. "They got to stop and blow those horses sometime. Where?"

Acosta did not hesitate in answering. "There's a place called Devil's Boulders. Maybe another ten, twelve miles along. They'll most likely try to make it down there ahead of nightfall. There's an old Indian corral of big stones with creek water running through it. If they don't stop there and rest those animals, come daylight we're goin' to be able to track them by dead horse carcasses." Gus spat and squinted ahead, then added, "Did you ever do anything like this before?"

Joe was peering southward through faint, smokelike waves of heat as he replied. "Couple of times years back, but we never caught up with them, and it was rustlers not horsethieves."

That seemed to satisfy the *remudero*. He was again straining to make out the dust banner as he said, "You ever been in New Mexico before?"

He hadn't. "No, pretty close to the line a few times but always on the Colorado side."

"Well, New Mexico's different, Joe."

Wryly Joe reached to rub the tip of his nose. "Yes it is for a damned fact!"

Gus turned to stare, but whatever curiosity Joe's sudden and very emphatic reply had aroused in him was left in abeyance as somewhere far ahead, the faint echo of one single gunshot sounded.

Gus said, "Hell," in a bitter, bleak voice. "They shot one. . . . Joe, I want those fellers. If we got to crawl on our bellies half the night to get close enough, I want them."

Acosta had made a good guess. As dusk was coming they passed a dead horse. It had been shot squarely between the eyes. It was an old mare, tucked up from hard running. Gus's jaw muscles rippled. "Sunflower. I watched her bein' born fifteen, eighteen years ago. I've broke six of her colts. She never made a mistake, Joe. Gentle and willing . . . " Acosta jettisoned his cud, blew his nose lustily and returned the old red bandana to a hip pocket. He said no more for a long while, but his dark profile spoke volumes.

Joe patted Red's neck. He was tiring but gallantly tried to conceal it. Joe looked back. There was no sign of Conley and the others. Anger surged in him. "What in hell are your friends doing back yonder, Gus? I'm not going to ride a good horse to death for some old bastard named Campbell I've never even seen, let alone a strawboss that's takin' his own sweet damned time."

Acosta came out of his bleak reverie with a hard look in Joe's direction. "I'll guess," he said, "they angled over to Springville."

Joe's color rose. "Springville, for Chris'sake!"

"To get Marshal Glover an' a posse. What we got to do is get up onto those thieves in the dark and hold them until the others get down here. It's the sensible thing to do — gettin' a posse I mean. I got no idea how many thieves are down there an' neither have you. I been watching tracks, an' every other horsethief I ever went after rode an animal with shoes. With these men you can't tell their animals from the loose stock. They sure as hell aren't apprentices at this business, Joe."

Joe's anger withered. He rode slowly until Gus led off in another lope, then he said, "Gus, you don't talk like any of the Mexicans I met up north."

Acosta looked across the intervening distance without smiling. "That's because I'm not a Mexican. I was born on the Texas border. My father had goats and raised gourds and peppers and maize. . . . *Bandeleros* came over the line in the night. . . . My mother hid me under an iron washtub. I was very young. Sometimes I still wake in the night hearing the gunshots, the yelling, my mother screaming. . . . Joe, I had one hell of a time pushing that tub over. It was iron and heavy as hell. . . . When I finally got out, it was just coming daybreak. My mother was dead, so was my father. Even our dog and some of the goats. We had two horses. They were gone. . . . Two days later some traders came by, took me along up into New Mexico and handed me over to some brothers at the San Felicidad mission near a town called Tanque Verde. They raised me. They almost never spoke Spanish an' they made me study. Ten years of that an' I couldn't even remember enough Spanish to ask for a drink of water. So I speak English . . . and Joe, I hate Mexicans. Especially if they wear shellbelts crossed over their chests. Any Mexicans . . . "

CHAPTER 9

Dark as Pitch

Acosta certainly knew the territory. As soft dusk thickened around them he turned off eastward. Joe, who had no idea where he was, made a point of remembering landmarks even though it occurred to him that he might never be down here again. He was thinking about that when Gus reined over closer at a walk and raised his arm.

Distant, but not so far away they could not be recognized for what they were, stood a jumble of bone-gray and weather-rounded ancient boulders. Some were nearly as tall as a mounted man, others were much smaller, and all of them were scattered within a hundred-yard radius. Joe studied them, then turned to look elsewhere for additional boulders. There were none, and he had seen none on the way down here. Another time and under different circumstances he would have pondered on this mystery of huge boulders which were far too heavy to have been brought here, being in an area which had no other rocks in any direction for as far as a man could see in broad daylight.

Gus spoke in needlessly hushed tones while continuing to point, moving his arm from side to side. "The tracks fan out a little but I'd guess the riders had 'em under good control." His arm dropped back to his side; his voice was tinged now with a steely tenseness. "We got them, Joe. . . . You smell smoke?"

Joe smelled nothing but his horse. Gus smiled icily. "We better leave the horses and do the rest of this on foot. Take along your saddlegun and pray those horses down yonder don't smell these horses. That's why I want to leave them this far from the rocks."

Joe looked down his nose at the shorter and darker man and could not resist being sarcastic. "Really? I thought maybe you liked crawling instead of riding."

But sarcasm was lost on Gonsalvo Acosta.

Gus remained with the horses for a long while, clearly waiting for it to get darker. It was open country between the place where they had tied the horses and those big rocks. Joe hunkered in thoughtful silence; he thought he was in good company for what they both might become involved in.

"I wish we was in the rocks and they was

out in the open," said Acosta.

Joe nodded. "Yeah. If wishes were horses a hell of a lot of poor people would ride, wouldn't they?"

Acosta flashed white teeth in the gloom, then turned back to studying the rocks. "They're cooking something," he said. "You smell it?"

This time Joe could smell smoke, so he nodded. "Maybe they feel pretty safe. I don't think they saw us comin' behind them. Otherwise they wouldn't be having supper."

A man's rough laughter came across through the darkening evening. Joe relaxed a little, more convinced than before that the horsethieves had no idea anyone was stalking them. Another man spoke loudly. Joe listened, then turned his head slowly. Gus was sitting motionless, scowling. Joe said, "Mexicans, hell — those are *gringos*."

Gus finally arose and walked back beyond the horses. During his absence there was an exchange of shouted insults from the area encircled by the largest boulders. Joe tipped back his hat, looking around for Acosta. When he finally returned, Joe said, "*Gringos*, Gus, and my guess is maybe four or five of them."

As he finished speaking another man spoke

loudly and this time it was in Spanish. A second man answering him in the same language. Gus hunkered back down wagging his head. He said nothing.

Joe was tiring of the wait. It was dark now, and it didn't look like the horsethieves were going to leave soon. They were going to stay the night.

He mentioned this to Gus and got a vigorous shake of the head unaccompanied by any words. Gus was clearly not interested in waiting until help arrived. Joe looked at him and sighed. They had accomplished their purpose; if Gus had some inherent need to fight horsethieves it might be commendable, but Joe Bryan saw no reason to try this alone, without the posse. He had as little use for horsethieves — thieves of any kind — as the next man, but getting shot at and possibly hit when there might not be any need to take such a risk left him mildly disgruntled.

The noise over in the rough circle of big rocks subsided. Even the smoke scent diminished. Gus tapped Joe's arm and without looking at him rose and started silently forward clutching his saddlegun.

Joe got up reluctantly to follow. A horse nickered among the rocks and Gus dropped flat against the ground. Joe did the same, but kept his head raised. No one came out of the rocks and the horse did not nicker a second time. Gus got up into a low crouch and started forward again. Joe did the same. They had covered about a hundred and fifty feet when someone ahead in the moonless night whistled loudly.

This time Joe flattened on the ground before his companion did, and this time his heart was pounding. The whistle had sounded to Joe like an alarm signal.

Nothing happened, but Joe did not move. He tried to make out a human silhouette in front of the rocks, or even in among them. He was sure the horsethieves had posted a sentinel, and he was almost certain this man had spotted them.

Gus turned his head to whisper. "Split up. You go west. I'll go east."

Joe watched the *remudero* slink away. The damned fool actually enjoyed this. Joe went in the opposite direction, treading very cautiously and listening for any kind of a sound. Whoever had whistled did not repeat it. Joe paused at least three hundred yards to the west before turning southward. Now, at last, he could detect the faint scent of cooking. It reminded him that breakfast had been a long time ago. He sank to one knee leaning on his

Winchester as he looked in the direction of the boulders. A horse squealed irritably and someone hawked and spat.

He was leaning to rise when what he thought was smoke seemed to drift out of the rocks in his direction. But this shadowy creation did not diminish in substance; it became more solid and distinguishable as it moved westward.

It was a man of average height and spare build. Joe felt his heart pick up its beat a little. The man was hatless. He did not appear to be fearful or watchful as he headed for a shallow little gully. What Joe particularly wished he had enough light to see was the man's middle. He did not believe the man was armed. He thought he knew why the man was walking so far from the camp.

The man halted once looking back, then he lighted a cigarette and in brilliant matchlight Joe saw his face. He was not a Mexican. The light guttered before it was possible to make out anything else. The tip of his quirley glowed brilliantly as he sucked in smoke, then grew dull as the man exhaled and continued toward the little arroyo.

Joe was less than forty feet from the arroyo's edge in a patch of short, sparse grass, no trees, no rocks, not even any sagebrush to use for concealment. If by chance the horsethief studied his terrain as he approached the edge of the gully, he could hardly avoid seeing the kneeling man with the carbine.

Joe dug in his left boot and eased his weight up. He could not possibly spring atop the horsethief even if he waited until the man went down into the arroyo. The distance was far too great.

Two horses squealed irritably at one another. Joe did not move his eyes; the oncoming horsethief ignored the sound.

The man walked right over the sloping lip of the gully and went down it without looking ahead or anywhere else. Joe left his pent-up breath out slowly and silently, gripped the gun and stalked the man.

The horsethief was standing with his back to Joe, smoking. He was going to finish his cigarette first. Joe crept to the very edge of the arroyo and without noise eased his Winchester around and leveled it at the unsuspecting horsethief. For Joe Bryan, everything had stopped, including time. He could whisper his command to the horsethief and not be heard as far as the field of boulders, but what the horsethief might do was unpredictable. If he cried out . . .

Joe did not even whisper, he simply cocked

the carbine. That small sound of oiled steel clicking over oiled steel was unmistakable. There was no other sound like it, and once a man had heard it he had no difficulty identifying it.

The horsethief's hand was in midair and it stopped there.

Joe whispered. "Turn around and don't make a damned sound."

The horsethief had recovered from his shock. He turned slowly, making a point of keeping both hands away from his sides, but Joe could see he was not armed. He and the horsethief stared at one another until Joe gestured for the man to lie face-down on the ground. "Flat down," he whispered.

The outlaw obeyed and as Joe arose from the west side of the little swale the man's head came up off the ground to watch his captor approach.

Joe moved toward the prone figure head-on. The Winchester was in his right hand, hanging at his side, when the horsethief sprang up off the ground. Joe flung up the carbine but did not quite get his free hand on it before the horsethief bowled into him with his head down like a charging bull.

Joe felt bone strike his Winchester as he was driven backward. The horsethief must have had a skull of solid bone: although he had collided with the Winchester head-on, he did not even stagger.

Joe dodged left, and as the horsethief came around he shifted to his right. Then he swung the Winchester like a club and the horsethief took the blow in the side and gasped. But he backed away and did not fall even though he was injured.

Joe dropped the Winchester and bulled ahead. The injured man had courage. Gasping with pain, he brought up his fists, but he had been hurt too badly to make a real battle of it. Joe Bryan knew what to do. He feinted to get the horsethief to raise his arms to protect his face, then landed a brutal blow to the horsethief's unprotected middle.

This time the man's breath rushed out and his legs turned loose. He fell to his knees and hung there, head hanging, arms clutching his middle as he fought to regain his breath. Joe thought he resembled a gut-shot bear.

CHAPTER 10

The Field of Boulders

Joe used the groaning man's belt to lash both arms in back, and used his own belt to truss the man's feet. Then he rummaged until he found the outlaw's soiled old bandana and knelt to gag him. When their eyes met, the outlaw gasped, "You son-of-a-bitch." Joe looked a long time into the lean, darkly tanned face.

"I could have killed you," Joe whispered, neither angry nor particularly upset. "That's what usually happens to horsethieves."

The injured man's glare did not diminish. "You knew better," he rasped. "A shot would have brought everyone out."

Joe nodded. "Yep. But mister, I was thinkin' more about cutting your damned throat. That's noiseless."

"I don't see no knife."

Joe raised his right trouser-leg and drew forth the wicked-bladed boot-knife he'd been carrying for the last ten years.

The outlaw's eyes jumped from the blade to Joe's cold smile, and didn't say a word. Joe pressed the knife tip to the bound man's throat.

"What's your name?"

The outlaw hung fire so Joe drew a speck of blood. He got immediate cooperation.

"Name's Henry Eustice."

"How many men are over in the rocks?"

"Six. Not countin' me, five."

Joe grunted. He gagged the horsethief and arose looking in the direction of the boulders.

The horsethief made fierce but undistinguishable sounds.

Joe nodded. "Lie easy, Henry. Try to relax and get some rest. And if you figure a way to spit out that gag and start yelling, you're dead."

He edged out of the little arroyo. There was no sign of Acosta. Even the corralled stolen horses seemed at last to be sleeping. The silence was deep and solid. Joe listened for riders coming down from the north and heard nothing at all.

Something slithered on his left and eastward a few yards. Joe swung the carbine in the direction of the sound, then he saw the lumpy dark shape of Acosta rising off the ground. Joe did not have to see the face;

Acosta's build was unique. He lowered the carbine as the *remudero* came up and looked past at the man in the swale. "Got one, eh?" he whispered, and turned his attention elsewhere, dismissing the prisoner that easily. "One man can ease down the three log poles keepin' the horses in that old stone pen. But when he does that an' the horses bust out, they're going to make enough noise to roust out everyone for a mile."

Joe muttered, "How many did you see?"

"Couldn't get into the rocks that well. I saw what I think was one man in a bedroll, but it's dark as hell and they're in among a lot of big rocks. . . . Joe, if you stalk up to the edge of the rocks on this side, I'll go back around and turn the horses loose on the other side."

"Then what?"

"Run for it. Get back to the horses and head north until we run into Al and the others."

"Just run for it?"

"No; you're goin' to shoot the first man you see come up to his feet with a gun — then run for it."

Joe gazed thoughtfully at Gonsalvo Acosta. "Wait a spell, Gus, and we'd ought to have some help." Joe knew the minute he said it that he was going to get an exasperated glare, and he did. Acosta shook his head. "I'll go back now," he whispered, and slipped soundlessly away.

The outlaw in the swale was trying very hard to say something. Joe did not even look around. He speculated on how long it would take Gus to get back around the boulders, decided he had some time to kill and squatted down. Then someone among the rocks began growling orders. Joe's heart sank. Whoever was head buckaroo was telling the others it was time to ride.

Joe arose and started forward. He angled so as to have the protection of a massive gray granite plinth between himself and the outlaws. Wherever in hell Gus Acosta was now, he would be much closer to the outlaws than Joe was. If he had managed to get anywhere near the pen with the stolen horses in it, and those grumbling men found him, Gus was going to need some help.

Acosta's plan to free the horses was too time-consuming now. From here on only improvisation mattered. Joe was aiming directly for the big rock when someone spoke swiftly in rapid Spanish. A moment later there was a muzzle blast that sprayed red light in all directions for one second. The sound of that gunshot bounced among the rocks, startling horses and men alike.

Joe sprinted up to the rock and leaned against it to catch his breath. There were shouts and growls among the outlaws now. Someone yelled a question in English and got back a shrill but heavily accented reply. The Spanish-speaking horsethief had seen a man creeping toward the gate poles of the rock corral.

Now Joe could hear the outlaws as they boiled out of their bedrolls, grabbed weapons and raced in the direction of the corral. He eased around the curve of his boulder to peer beyond it. The width between his big rock and the one adjoining it was only a few inches, not enough room for a man to squeeze through but wide enough for Joe to see night-shapes running away from him. He raised his carbine and snapped a shot at the legs of a man who was dodging around a large rock. Pieces of shattered granite as sharp as knives flew in all directions. The man squawked and hurled himself out of sight beyond the big round stone.

Men cried out warnings and threw themselves behind whatever shelter was available. Joe dodged to the left, ducking as low as he could each time he had to pass an open place between the rocks.

Then there was silence. Joe halted in a squatting position behind a low, broad boulder. His intention had been to cause enough uproar to allow Gus time to get clear. By now Acosta should have gotten away. A man's voice called shrilly. "Henry? What the hell's goin' on out there?"

A second voice, deeper and gruffer, said, "It ain't Henry, for Chris'sake."

The silence ran on. Joe looked rearward. It was a long sprint to the horses, and while he did not feel that the surprised outlaws would stalk him until they knew a lot more, he was reluctant to leave shelter and start running.

But he did it, hoping very hard that his analysis of the outlaws' confusion and fear was correct. Evidently it was, because no one fired at him.

Gus was with the horses, peering into the dark at Joe. He thrust the sorrel's reins into Joe's hand and without a word sprang atop his own horse. Then he said, "They can't stay there. Follow me. We can get over on the east side and stay out aways to watch for them to try an' turn the horses out. We got to keep them from heading south again."

Joe's sorrel, tied long enough to be restless, had to be held back. Gus rode like a man who could see in the dark. He cantered in a large half-circle and did not halt until it was barely possible to see the boulder field. As he swung down, he pointed with the barrel of the carbine. "Past those round-topped big rocks is the poles they use for a gate."

Joe dropped off the left side of his horse with one split rein looped around the horn, the other one trailing through his fingers. He stared in the direction Gus had motioned. They were too far out to see shapes let alone movement. He started ahead leading his horse, not stopping until he thought it would be possible to see a man yanking down the poles. Then he knelt on one knee.

The outlaws were quiet, no doubt because someone had told them to be. Gus came up a couple yards to Joe's left and leaned his gun aside as he foraged for his cut plug. As he was shaving off a cud he muttered, "That stirred up a hornet's nest."

Joe did not look around. "Where in tarnation is Conley?"

Gus froze. "Listen!"

The sound was distant and barely audible but it was clearly made by a party of riders loping southward. Gus smiled in the darkness. "There's your answer."

Joe caught a flash of movement between the boulders and raised his Winchester, waited, and when nothing happened, he fired anyway. This time three guns fired back, making Gus and Joe dart sideways.

Joe shook his head. "They were waiting for that, Gus."

Acosta muttered something and faced northward where the sound of horsemen was becoming increasingly audible. He turned back and scowled in the direction of the rocks. "We can make a run at them on horseback an' fire between the rocks."

Joe turned slowly, carbine crooked into the bend of his left arm. "Are you crazy?" he asked. "They're not goin' to bust out of the rocks, Gus. All we got to do is wait."

"We could get it done before the others get down here," insisted the *remudero*.

Joe continued to gaze at his companion. "That's what they thought at the Alamo. Settle down."

The noise of loping horses was loud enough now to be heard very clearly. Joe watched the rocks. The forted-up outlaws were listening too.

Gus finally abandoned his notion of attacking the hidden outlaws, and led his horse away. When he was out a dozen or so yards he mounted and rode at a stiff trot in the direction of the advancing riders. Joe remained where he was.

He tied the sorrel and slipped up as close as he dared. The outlaws had three choices: Free the stolen horses and race for it, perhaps using the loose stock as their protective shield; remain forted up and try to fight off odds that were likely to be overpowering very shortly. Or, and this was why Joe was inching ahead in the darkness, the outlaws could abandon the stolen horses, sneak out of the rocks southward and make a wild break for it.

Joe halted to listen. The possemen and their companions were close enough now for the sound of rein chains to be heard. Gus would be meeting up with them soon.

He also heard something else, someone deep in the boulders swearing at a horse. Joe turned, swung up on the sorrel and pushed him over into a rocking-chair lope on an encircling course that would take him back around to where Gus and Joe had watched the corral earlier.

The outlaws had evidently decided to abandon the stolen livestock and try to save their skins. Joe continued to lope. Passing the place where he and Gus had waited, he rode southward another hundred or so yards then hauled back, slid to the ground and waited. It was a very brief wait. A man led his saddled horse out of the rocks to the south. He was treading warily, head swinging from left to right. Joe waited until he turned to toe into the stirrup, then fired a round directly in front of the horse. As bits of hard earth and small stones exploded no more than five feet from the horse's chest, peppering the animal, it flung up its head with a loud snort, yanked the reins out of the astonished man's hand, and ran.

Joe spurred the sorrel horse back the way he had come. Even so, angry gunmen fired around the entire area where they had seen Joe's muzzle blast. He had not expected them to respond that quickly.

The gunfire ended. Across its waning echoes, a bull-bass voice roared in the direction of the field of rocks. "This is Marshal Glover from Springville! Come out of them rocks an' leave your weapons behind. If you don't — there are men around your camp. When I yell, they're goin' to charge you. You hear me? There are fifteen of us."

Joe halted and turned back. He was too far away and it was too dark to see much more than ghostly shapes of big rocks. He waited for someone to yell, but no one did, so he walked the sorrel horse closer and halted again. He could see a little better but not very much, and going closer would put him in gun-range.

Marshal Glover called again, impatiently this time. "You don't have all night! Come out of those rocks or you're goin' get buried among them. I want to see you fellers comin' out. *Now!*"

Joe soft-walked his horse still closer. He was within gunrange, so he dismounted and held the Winchester in both hands waiting for whatever happened next. A thin voice called in fractured English. "Coming out, coming out! Now you don't shoot, all right?"

Glover's disgust had increased. "All right. No one is going to shoot. Walk northward until we can see you plain."

Joe waited, as did all the other horsemen. He saw a lean blurred shape creep among the foremost rocks. At the same moment the sorrel horse threw up its head, ears pointing southward. Joe said, "Hell," and reined down in that direction. The sorrel horse had been correct. It was not one man leading a horse out of the rocks as before, it was four men. Joe angled farther out, swung down and hoisted his carbine all in one smooth movement. This time he did not pick a target, he simply fired into the stony ground in front of the skulking outlaws and kept on firing until the Winchester was empty.

One outlaw managed to control his animal

and spring astride it. He was spurring wildly southward as the other outlaws continued to be dragged by their terrified mounts.

Someone spurred past, between Joe and the tangled outlaws and their frightened horses, in a belly-down run. Joe was up-ending the empty saddlegun into its boot and only caught a short glimpse of the speeding rider. But even in darkness, Joe recognized Gonsalvo Acosta. He grunted to himself, stepped astride and was reining directly toward the frantically struggling men and horse when a loose body of riders swept around from the west. Each man had a gun in his right hand.

Marshal Glover was in front. He drew rein and fired a pistol shot into the ground between his horse and the outlaws, then he bawled at them. "Let go of the horses and stand where you are. Keep your arms wide. *I said let the damned horses go!*"

Joe waited until he saw the outlaws begin to obey, freeing their frightened animals and lifting both arms away from their bodies. Then he turned southward and eased Red into a lope. He did not expect to overtake Gus and the one that got away. At least not until they stopped somewhere. But Joe wanted to back Gus. The horseless outlaws near the rocks had tried and lost; Marshal Glover would no longer need Joe Bryan, but there was a chance Gus might.

Over along the uneven, far curve of the world, a very pale, diluted streamer of dawn blue was limning crags and sawtooth ridges and raw granite a mile above timberline. Another day was arriving. Joe, as he rode along watching that cold, distant skyline, found it difficult to believe that the rock-field fight had used up an entire night.

He heard the very distant echo of a gunshot but did not have the heart to make his tired horse pick up the gait. But he rode standing in his stirrups trying to penetrate the paling distance from whence that gunshot had come.

CHAPTER 11

Another Day

It was a long ride and would have been longer if something hadn't made the fleeing man's horse pull up lame. The horse was what Joe saw first in the widening band of dawn. It was standing with reins hanging, favoring its off front leg.

Acosta's mount was off to the east — he'd taken time to hobble it. There was not even any decent underbrush down here to tie it to. The horse was muzzling for grass, though there was not very much of that either.

There was no sign of Gus or the other man. The land rolled more than it had back near the boulder field, and seemed to be flintier. There were swales and rolling long ribs of land, but no trees nor rocks.

As Joe swung off and dropped down to hobble Red, he heard a man shout, and the distant voice sounded like that of Gonsalvo Acosta.

Joe rose and stood in front of his sorrel

horse looking for Gus or the other man, and when he found no trace of either he called out too. "Gus! Let go a round in his direction and I'll get behind him."

Gus's shot cracked from the far side of a slight ridge roughly a hundred and fifty yards ahead. Before the echoes died another man yelled, but this time shrilly. "I quit. You fellers hear me? I said I quit!"

Gus snarled at the man. "Stand up with your arms straight out from your shoulders!"

After a few minutes of nothing happening Joe started to gather his reins to mount. Then a rather tall, lanky man came up off the ground up on the far side of the swale where Gus was crouched. He was holding both arms straight out to his sides from the shoulder.

Joe mounted, palmed his colt and started riding toward the area where he expected to find Gus. He got atop the rounded, gentle rim of the swale and looked down. Gus was not there. He looked elsewhere, and saw something furtive move against the ground near a sickly stand of blue sage growing in a clump. He kneed his horse out, riding directly toward the outlaw, ignoring what he knew: Gus was sneaking around the raised rim to be in position to aim well.

When Joe reached the outlaw, the man

looked upward with a twisted expression and said, "You ever try standin' with your arms out like this for long?"

"Lower them," Joe said after looking around toward the south end of the rim. He did not see Gus but knew he was there. He dismounted and stood on the left side of his horse as he eased ahead to get between the unarmed outlaw and the *remudero*.

That brought Gus to his feet angry as a hornet. He waved his Winchester and yelled. "Joe, get the hell out of the way."

Joe turned slowly, studied the barrel-shaped figure of Gus and said, "Cut it out, Gus. That's enough."

"Damn it, get out of the way, Joe!"

"Nope. You're goin' to have to shoot through me."

The outlaw's voice cracked in fear: "What more does he want? I left the guns on the ground, I give up!"

Joe answered without looking at the man. "He wants to kill you. He hates horse-thieves."

"Don't let him. Mister, don't let him do it!"

Joe continued to ignore the horsethief. He said, "Gus — leave it be. They'll likely hang him anyway, an' if you shoot him — him being unarmed — Glover'll peel hide off you an inch at a time. . . . Gus?"

The *remudero* grounded his carbine, glared and growled a curse. He was so disgusted that he refused to walk up to them but turned and went around the lip of the swale, marching in the direction of his horse.

The outlaw's breath came out raggedly. "Close," he muttered.

Joe agreed as he faced the man. "Yeah. You got a name?"

"Quite a few."

"How about the one you were born with?"

The outlaw was as tall as Joe but not as broad. He eyed his captor from sardonic dark eyes. Joe prompted him. "I could have let him shoot you. Maybe I'll do it myself."

"Mark Lawyer."

Joe looked skeptically at the man. The outlaw looked straight back. "That's the truth."

Joe said, "What happened to your horse?"

"He was runnin' hard, stepped into a little hole and wrenched his ankle. Otherwise that Mex wouldn't have come close."

Joe gestured. "Walk out where your horse is. When we start back you can lead it."

The horsethief trudged up out of the swale with Joe twenty feet to the rear. When they were back on level ground they could see Gus far out with his horse and Joe's sorrel. They also saw the animal with a badly swollen ankle.

Daylight was over the land, the chill of very early morning was fading, and a mile or more northward two mounted men were walking their horses without haste in Joe's and Gus's direction. The outlaw hesitated as he saw them, evidently recognized them as strangers, and resumed plodding along. Gus mounted and led Joe's sorrel by the reins as he rode toward them.

When they reached the lame horse Joe stepped aside to examine the injury. It was a bad sprain but nothing was broken. The horse would recover but it would take many months. The outlaw ignored everything but Gus Acosta, riding toward them with a carbine balanced across his lap, dark eyes fixed in turn on the horsethief. The outlaw finally said, "Pardner, he's going to try it again."

Joe stood up looking around. "I don't think so," he murmured.

The outlaw stiffened and glared. "You don't think so!"

Joe nodded. "I don't give a damn, but I don't think he'll try it. That big man on the bay horse north of us is the lawman from Springville. Gus may hate your guts, mister, but he don't hate them enough to commit murder with a lawman lookin' on. . . . Sit down."

The outlaw obeyed and as Gus rode up looking murderous, Joe said, "Put up the Winchester."

Gus turned his fierce eyes to Bryan. "Don't tell me what to do!"

Joe smiled. "Yeah, I will, Gus. . . You put up that gun or I'll do it for you."

Acosta's fierce glare deepened right up until Joe started toward him. Then Gus upended the carbine and let it slide into its boot. He dismounted and spoke bitterly. "One less horsethief in this world would be a blessing."

Joe did not disagree with that. What he disagreed with was cold-blooded killing. He did not reply but turned to watch Glover and a spare, permanently tanned older man ride up and halt. The older man had a face like a relief map of the badlands. He leaned on the saddlehorn listening to Gus explain who their captive was and how he had made a break for it. Then the older man drifted his gaze to Joe Bryan and said, "I'm James Campbell. Al Conley told me about you."

Joe waited for the rest of it but the older man turned his attention to the horsethief when he spoke again. "Stand up. Now then, we got your friends and I got my *remuda* back." Old Campbell looked craggy and unforgiving. Joe glanced at Glover, hoping to find something in the big lawman's face to indicate that he would not stand for an execution. What he saw was an identical look of hatred.

Campbell spoke again to the outlaw. "No trees handy so I expect we'd better head back where there are some. Get on your horse."

Joe said, "The horse has a sprained ankle, Mister Campbell."

Old Campbell did not even look at the horse. "Then start walking, and lead the horse. . . . Gus, did you look for a belly gun or a boot knife?"

Gus shook his head. "I didn't search him. How about you, Joe?"

"Nope. There's a six-gun an' a Winchester lying in the gravel on the far side of the swale. He told me he didn't have any other weapons."

Marshal Glover dismounted and approached the horsethief. Their faces were less than ten inches apart when Glover snarled. "You got a belly gun or a boot knife — or any kind of a weapon?"

Lawyer met the black glare for a moment or two, then skipped his gaze elsewhere, but there were no friendly faces so he said, "Yeah, a boot knife." He leaned down and pulled up his trouser leg until his captors could see the flattened horn handle.

"Shuck it," snarled Glover. As the knife fell in the grass, Marshal Glover completed the job with a rough personal search and pushed his big hand in Joe's direction with a snub-nosed under-and-over forty-one caliber belly gun on his palm. Then he went back to his horse in disgust and motioned northward. "Start walking."

Joe and Gus brought up the rear. Gus wagged his head, spat amber and looked over at his companion. "He'd have found a way. He'd have shot you or knifed you. And you didn't think I should kill him."

James Campbell twisted to look back at Joe. "How old are you?"

"Crowding forty."

"How in hell have you managed to live that long?" the cowman exclaimed, squared around and rode onward beside Marshal Glover.

Joe, his face red, considered the older man's back. Gus looked pleased as he went to work on his cut plug.

It was a long ride and by the time they got back to the rocks, the sun was climbing, heat was building up and the rock field was deserted. Evidently the rangemen and possemen had struck out for town with their prisoners — all but one. As Joe followed Glover and Campbell past the rocks he saw a fresh mound of boulders in the middle of the corral made of piled rocks. Gus saw it too. He chewed and said nothing.

When they were far enough up-country to head for that creek where Joe and Gus had tanked up yesterday, Glover reined over.

The captured horsethief was trudging almost stoically, his shirt dark with sweat. His injured horse was moving better than it had been but it still had a bad limp. Joe thought a little of the swelling had gone down.

As they swung off to hobble the horses, Campbell led his animal to the creek beside Joe's sorrel. He watched his horse and seemed preoccupied. As Joe was turning his horse away from the water Campbell spoke to him. "I owe you thanks for keepin' at it on your first day as one of my riders. We usually don't have to do things like this and a lot of men wouldn't have stayed on."

Joe regarded the older man across his saddleseat. James Campbell was old, but except for his face he did not look it, and Joe thought he probably did not act like it. He had run across these rawhide-tough old stockmen before, and almost invariably if they were single they were curt, cantankerous and tough to get along with. He still had forty-five dollars in the moneybelt under his shirt. "It's not running down horsethieves that makes me think I shouldn't have hired on, Mister Campbell."

The old man's steely eyes came around, as steady as wet rocks and about as hard. "But you did hire on."

"Sure did, an' it won't take any more time to quit than it did to hire on."

The granitelike eyes did not blink. "I told you we don't do things like — "

"I said that wasn't it, Mister Campbell. . . . I met an old bronco in the mountains my first day in your country and he told me you were a mean man to get along with."

"What . . . Who was he?"

"It doesn't matter. You can pay me wages for one day or you can forget it."

Glover and Gus were standing nearby elaborately busy with their horses, listening to every word. Even the outlaw was listening.

James Campbell stood looking steadily at Joe Bryan for a long time, then grunted and led his horse back from the willows into sunshine. Glowering at the lawman and Gus, he snugged up his cinch. When Joe followed with the sorrel, there was the prisoner, his boots and socks off. His pale feet were pink and swollen. Joe said, "Go soak 'em in the creek. We'll wait."

The outlaw hunkered down and gasped as his feet came into contact with the water, but he held them in.

Gus was uncomfortable. So was Henry Glover. James Campbell looked from Joe to the outlaw seated on grassy creekbank. Campbell seemed undecided about whether to wait or to head for town. He waited, but he took Henry Glover out a hundred yards and they talked. Gus Acosta glanced sideways at Joe and said, "He don't mean anything. That's just his way."

Joe's answer was short. "Yeah, I know. And that was just my way too. Gus, I was lookin' for a job when I met you fellers on the stageroad yesterday, and I'll still be lookin' for one tomorrow."

Gus did not yield. "He's good to work for, Joe."

"I guess so or you wouldn't have stayed with him so long, but he doesn't need me any more'n I need him."

"You're too touchy, Joe."

Joe did not argue. "Maybe. And maybe he's mad because two of his riders jumped me in town and got the worst of it when the marshal stepped in. Gus, if I stayed on I'd have trouble with those two sure as hell."

"Naw, you wouldn't. You're talkin' about Hudson and Kinkaid. When they got back and told their story at supper, the old man raised the roof and threatened to fire them if they ever do anything that childish again when they're in town. Anyway, I've ridden with Jim Kinkaid an' Jack Hudson. They don't carry grudges. Besides, the way they told it, you didn't do anything; it was the marshall who did it."

Joe regarded the *remudero's* dark, coarse features. Except for wanting to charge up guns blazing and attack six outlaws last night, Gus seemed to be easy-going. Probably if there were no horsethieves or Mexicans to upset him, Gus Acosta would be a good man to ride the rims with.

Campbell and the marshal were walking back so Joe called to the man at the creek. When they were ready to continue toward town the outlaw had noticeably less trouble leading his lame horse.

After two miles and with the sun almost directly above them, the outlaw lifted his hat, mopped sweat, resettled the hat and caught Joe watching him.

They were all hungry and at least three of

them were tired. Joe also itched. He thought of the zinc bathtub in his sister's kitchen and imagined himself lolling in it for a solid hour.

Campbell raised an arm. There were big trees up ahead about where Springville was. They still had a few miles to go but the worst was behind them — for all of them except the horsethief. He eyed the town up ahead with a lot less enthusiasm than his companions had.

CHAPTER 12

Bryan's Luck

When the possemen and rangemen had returned to Springville — hours before the last horsethief arrived in town with his mounted escort — the prisoners had been locked up and the riders had gone to the saloon, so when Joe, Gus and the others rode in, there were spectators on both sides of the road.

Joe left them at the livery barn. He handed over the reins to a large, red-faced fat man this time. There was no sign of the wispy hostler. He told the fat man how he wanted his animal cared for and the fat man got redder by the moment as he listened. He was chewing the stub of an unsmoked cigar which he finally removed as he put a sulphurous glare upon Joe and said, "Cowboy, I been carin' for horses since before you was born."

Joe considered the thick bloated red face. "Maybe you have, but this horse gets what he damned well needs."

The liveryman gazed at his cigar stub.

"Maybe you better take him somewhere else," he said, and raised his eyes.

Joe blew out a long breath as he regarded the fat man. He hadn't slept nor eaten since yesterday, and he had been humiliated by an old leather-necked cowman. Without moving his feet he swung hard and the fat man went over backward in a bleating heap.

Joe waited for him to flounder over onto all fours and push himself back upright. Joe saw that wispy old hostler come into view looking startled. He ignored him and smiled at the fat man. "I don't think I'll take him somewhere else. I think you'll cuff him good, give him a stall with clean straw in it, grain him, feed him a big flake of decent hay, an' when I come back if he isn't happy and shiny, I'm going to worry about fifty pounds off you."

The fat man had the back of one hand to a small bleeding place on the left side of his mouth. His anger was gone, his eyes were wide and glassy. He nodded his head.

Joe walked up to the café. The proprietor stared at him. He was unshaven, gaunt and sunken-eyed, and his clothing was rumpled and dirty. He ignored the stare to ask if the caféman had any supper left. The older man nodded. "I'll fill a platter. First, you look like you need coffee."

Joe sipped the hot coffee and looked around. The café was empty. It was the wrong time of day for customers. He settled forward and nursed the coffee until his meal arrived then he went to work with both hands while the caféman loitered, slapping at flies with an old dishtowel. Joe ignored him until he had finished and arose to count out the coins. Then he said, "Is that fat man at the livery barn the owner?"

The caféman nodded. "Yeah. Bud Hickson."

"Disagreeable cuss, isn't he?"

The caféman spread his hands. "Bud froze his feet a long time ago. It's hard for him to get around and sometimes they pain him something awful."

Joe nodded and as he turned he said, "He's got a lip that'll take his mind off his feet," and walked out into the roadway leaving the caféman staring after him.

The only person at the jailhouse was Marshal Glover. Everyone else was up at the saloon. Glover glanced up as the door opened, then glanced down again. He was laboriously writing names and dates in a dog-eared gray ledger. "Have a seat," he said and went on working.

Joe got comfortable. There were six Winchesters, two shotguns — one sawed off so that the barrel was no more than fifteen inches long — and three six-guns in a rack along the rear wall. To the left of the rack was a large army cannon stove. Beside it on the floor were a dozen and a half split rounds, neatly stacked.

Marshal Glover shoved the ledger aside, clasped both hands atop his table and leaned forward, looking at his visitor. He wagged his head a little as he spoke. "You and Gus earned your keep."

Joe let his gaze drift around to the marshal's face. "Yeah. What happened after I left the boulders?"

Glover looked at his big clasped hands. "We had 'em all out front on foot. Well, we thought we had 'em all out there." Glover's hard gaze lifted. "We didn't know you'd already caught one in that swale west of the rocks. He got loose."

Joe stared.

"And — he snuck over to the rocks to find a horse."

Joe got a sour sensation in the pit of his stomach. "And got shot? I saw a burial cairn when we rode past the rocks."

"Well, yes, he got shot, but one of their horses ran back into the stone pen. Al Conley went to catch it. That feller you tied up had a six-gun. I got no idea where he got it, maybe out of his bedroll or maybe from a saddlebag. . . . We were outside of the rocks with the captives and this skulkin' one came in after that horse. I don't think Al knew he was there, but maybe he did because his gun was on the ground when we got up there. . . . Anyway, that horsethief went for the horse and shot Conley. . . . He got the horse, too, and made a run for it. Feller named Jim Kinkaid, you remember him? He knelt, tracked the outlaw with his Winchester an' shot him out of the saddle. Killed him deader'n a stone."

"Conley?"

Marshal Glover looked down at his big clasped hands again. "Dead when we got up there. Right through the brisket. The others brought him up with them when they headed for town with the outlaws — all but the one we piled rocks on, and the one you and Gus cornered. By any chance do you know the name of that feller you tied up in the swale?"

"He said his name was Henry Eustice," Joe replied, turning slightly to gaze into the space between his chair and the cannon stove. "Why didn't you or Mister Campbell tell us about Conley on the ride back?"

"Well, Al was his tophand. It was up to him and he didn't seem to want to talk about it. They was good friends, Mister Campbell and Al Conley. . . . He was a nice feller — Conley, I mean. Never caused any trouble in town, was good-natured most of the time. Easy to be around."

Joe nodded. That had been pretty much the way he would have described the tophand, and he hadn't really known him very well. He said, "How about the others?"

"Down in my cells. Tomorrow I'll go through the dodgers. Sure as hell they're wanted somewhere."

The door burst open and the fat liveryman rushed in, took one look at Joe Bryan, gulped like a fish out of water, then turned and fled back out to the roadway leaving Marshal Glover staring round-eyed at the open door. Joe leaned and gave it a push to close it. To clarify things he said, "I took my horse to him when we got to town. I told him how I wanted it cared for. That's a good horse, a friend of mine. He didn't like some unwashed cowboy telling him how to care for a horse — so I knocked him down. That's what he was going to complain to you about until he saw me sitting here."

Marshal Glover's gaze drifted back to the

door briefly. "You got to understand about Bud. He — "

"Froze his feet once and they bother him. I know. The caféman told me. Marshal, maybe it's me and maybe it's you folks. I didn't know he had sore feet and I didn't know why Mister Campbell was so riled up. Nobody told me. Now, in my boots, how would you have reacted to both those men?"

Glover was back gazing at his big clasped hands again, and his reply was slow arriving. "It does seem that somehow you manage to get off on the wrong foot, don't it? Like Kinkaid and Jack Hudson in front of the saloon day before yesterday."

Joe looked steadily at the big man. "*I* don't get off on the wrong foot, Marshal. I was minding my own business when Kinkaid and Hudson thought they'd choose a stranger. As for the fat man and Campbell — they got tongues, haven't they?"

Glover turned his gaze on Bryan. He leaned back in his chair, his eyes unmoving. "It's strange for a fact, Mister Bryan. The more I sit here an' think about it, the stranger it seems."

"What does?"

"It's sort of like you're hung with bad luck."

Joe began to scowl. "Marshal — how come it's always me and no one else?"

Glover continued to loll back in his chair gazing at the rangeman. "You know why I didn't go up to the saloon? Jim Campbell asked me along. I wanted to go. I also wanted to step over to the café. I'm hungry as a nursing sow bear."

Joe sat patiently waiting for wherever all this was going to end, and the longer Marshal Glover deliberated and philosophized before getting down to brass tacks, the more that sinking sensation began to trouble Joe's stomach again.

Glover heaved his bulk forward in the chair, picked a paper off a random, untidy pile of other papers and studied it in solemn silence for a while. Then he tossed it to the edge of his desk and said, "That's why I was still sittin' in here writing the names and charges of those outlaws in my office book when you came along. . . . You know what that is? Well, I've only seen one of those things before in my life, and so I was sittin' here tryin' to make up my mind what to do about it."

Joe straightened in the chair. "What is it?"

"Read it. Help yourself. It's a federal form Indian agents and sometimes U.S. marshals fill out." Glover paused to watch Joe reach, pick up the paper and settle back back in his chair to read it. "I knew you had a kid when you rode into Springville. I was told she's up at your sister's place right now."

Joe raised hard eyes. "Not she — he. It's a little boy."

Glover accepted that in stride. "He — I saw you with him at the café. . . . That paper was under the office door when I opened up after we got back today. It's a signed federal order for you to turn over to the local Indian agent — he's about sixteen miles from town southeast on the reservation — one Indian child you got no right to."

Joe read in bleak silence, then held up the paper for better light and reread it. He had never seen such a document, had in fact never known such a document existed. As he lowered it, Glover, watching his face, forced an uncomfortable smile and said, "See what I mean? Bad luck sticks to you like a woodtick."

Joe flipped the paper back onto the untidy desk. "Who signed that thing?"

Glover flicked a glance at the paper. He had already read it several times. "The signature is genuine. Frank Beale is the Indian agent."

"Marshal, how did he know I even existed,

let alone that I had a little boy with me?"

Glover shrugged massive shoulders. "I got no idea. Well, I shouldn't quite say that. There are plenty of folks around who got no use for Indians, even little ones. My guess is that someone from town went down to the reservation in the past few days and told Mister Beale you had the child."

Joe wished he had gone to the saloon instead of coming here. Not simply because this new trouble upset him, but because right now he needed a couple of jolts of old popskull.

Marshal Glover looked almost sympathetic, which was something he had not been toward the horsethieves. He said, "That amounts to an order to me to round up the little boy and deliver him to the reservation."

Joe shoved out both legs and studied the scuffed toes of his boots. "Is this some kind of a law, Marshal?"

"Afraid so. They're not supposed to be off the reservation. If they go off, someone usually sends out one of those papers so's the law has to find them and take them back. Mister Bryan, do you mind tellin' me what happened to his mother?"

Joe stared at the large man. "You think I'm his father?"

"Well now, aren't you? Why else would you

be traipsing around the country takin' him with you?"

Joe went back to gazing at his boot-toes. "He's not a fullblood, Marshal. I've seen 'breed Indians in just about every town I've been in and no one made them go to a — "

"Fine. Now prove to me he's not a fullblood. Mister Bryan, if you do that, I can write on this paper he's not a reservation Indian and that ought to end it. You want to prove it?"

Joe shoved up out of the chair and reset his hat. "No. Right now I want a bath, a change of clothes and time to sit somewhere quiet and think about this." He went to the door and as his hand touched the latch Marshal Glover stood up behind his big table.

"Mister Bryan, I'm caught in the middle. I got this damned paper to execute. . . . If you walk out of my office now and go up to your sister's place, wrap the child up, get on your horse and ride all night. . . . You see what I'm getting at?"

"Not exactly. But I'm not going to make a run for it if that's what's bothering you."

Glover stood at the desk looking steadily at Joe Bryan. "I know you believe in right an' wrong, otherwise you wouldn't have bought into Campbell's trouble with those horsethieves. So — you pass me your word you'll come here to this office in the morning with the little boy, and I'll let you walk out of here right now. Otherwise I'd have to lock you up an' go get the little boy an' lock him up too."

Joe stared. Marshal Glover glanced at the top of his untidy desk, then up again. "You think *you* don't like this? Take my word for it, I don't like it neither. But I got my job to do. Do I have your word?"

Joe nodded stiffly. "You got it," he said. He walked out of the jailhouse and turned north in the direction of his sister's cottage without seeing any of the people who gazed at him with interest: they had heard about his part in the capture of those horsethieves. This gawd-damned New Mexico country had it in for him — somehow, he thought bitterly.

CHAPTER 13

Henry Glover's Complication

Wes was in bed and Mary Jane laced hot coffee for her brother as she listened silently to everything he had to say about what was now common knowledge around town — the fight at the boulder field, the killing of Mister Campbell's tophand and the return to town with the captives. He did not mention the federal order Marshal Glover had shown him.

Mary was sympathetic, helped him haul water for a bath and heated it on the woodstove while he was out back shaving. Afterward, she left him to scrub and soak, and think. Twice he nearly fell asleep in the tub, so he dried off, emptied the tub out back in the geranium bed and went off to bed.

He did not awaken until the sun was climbing and the aroma of frying sidemeat filled the house, that and boiling coffee.

By the time he got out to the kitchen, Wes

had been fed and was already out back inside the fence working with fierce concentration on a project he had started the day before: he was creating a hiding place with walls of crate slats and a roof of grass tufts for concealment. Joe went out there and Wes ran to him, shiny-eyed, and tugged at his hand to show him the fruit of his labor. Joe knelt down and solemnly examined everything. Wes fidgeted while awaiting the man's judgment. Joe finally looked around and winked. "Couldn't have done better myself," he said, and Wes was delighted.

Mary called Joe to breakfast. As he returned to the house he decided to ride down to the Indian reservation and hunt up the man named Beale who had signed that order. During the course of their running conversation as he ate, Joe asked his sister if she had ever heard of a man named Beale. She turned from the stove gazing at him. "Frank Beale, the Indian agent?"

"That's the one. You ever heard of him?"

"Joe, six months after Wes died he started coming by. Sometimes with candy, sometimes with magazines or flowers."

Joe pushed the empty plate aside and pulled in his coffee cup. "Do you like him, Mary?"

She turned her back to him and became

busy at the stove as she answered. "He seemed nice at first. Considerate and all. Offered to help me any way he could."

Joe sipped coffee. Years earlier he had been able to pretty well understand his sister from what she did *not* say about people and things. He considered the cup's black contents. "But you aren't exactly fond of him."

She turned. "He already has one wife, Joe."

Joe nodded and put the cup aside. "I got to go see him, Mary."

She stared. "What about?"

He went to the stove to refill the cup before answering. When he was back at the table he explained everything Marshal Glover had told him last night. She leaned on the stove, and when that failed to provide the support she needed she went to the table and dropped down opposite her brother, face pale, eyes dark with foreboding. When he had finished she almost whispered, "You can't let them take Wes."

He gazed broodingly at her, then smiled and leaned to pat her hand. "I don't figure to."

"What else did Henry Glover say?"

"Well, not much more than what I just told you. Except that he's not real happy to be in the middle."

"Joe, Henry knows the law. He'd ought to be able to do more than just wring his hands."

He smiled softly at her. "Mary, he has his job. I'd guess there are times when he hates having to do it. Not just in this case."

She left the room with watery eyes. The last view Joe had of her was that of a woman holding back tears.

He arose to look out the back door where the little boy was burrowing and grunting, and scuffing dirt like a busy badger, copper toe-caps still shiny.

He went through the house for his shellbelt and hat then left by the front door. The sun was climbing, Springville was busy and lively, there was not a cloud in the sky.

Someone spoke his name from the roadway. Three horsemen were out there: Mister Campbell and those two riders of his who had tried to provoke Joe in front of the saloon, Hudson and Kinkaid. Campbell had called his name again and was now reining over toward the plankwalk where he halted, leaned on the saddlehorn looking steadily at Joe Bryan as he said, "Nice day."

Joe nodded and looked at the riders behind Campbell. "Very nice. Might be nicer if there was a few clouds up there."

Campbell's eyes barely twinkled in appreciation of the professional rangeman's view that sunshine should be followed very soon by rain. He let a moment pass then said, "You had breakfast, Mister Bryan?"

Joe studied the craggy, lined, dark leathery face. "About an hour back."

"I see. Well, would you care for a drink at the saloon?"

Joe slowly shook his head. "Not much of a drinkin' man, Mister Campbell." It had become increasingly obvious that this probably was no accidental meeting, and that Campbell had something on his mind. Joe's bafflement lifted slightly; he thought the cowman had hunted him up to pay him one day's wages.

Campbell looked up and down the roadway, then back at the man in overhang shade on the plankwalk. Joe thought he would help the older man so he said, "If it's about payin' me for yesterday . . ."

Campbell's piercing eyes did not move from Joe's face or blink. He had lived a long time, knew men, was a master at situations and right now he thought he had correctly gauged the muscular man in front of him, so he tried what usually worked with stockmen: humor. He said, "I was a little short with you yestiddy. Mister Bryan, a man gets old. You'll understand that. . . . Y'see when a man's mean and ugly, though, folks don't notice the change as he gets older."

The twinkle in the cowman's gaze made Joe respond with a smile, then he laughed. Kinkaid and Hudson also laughed and Jim Campbell swung to the ground, handed his reins to Jack Hudson and still with the twinkle stepped up onto the duckboards as he tugged off his riding gloves. "How about a game of pool, if you got somethin' against a drink this early in the day?"

Joe was almost ready to like this James Campbell, who was different from yesterday's James Campbell. "I'd take you on except that I got something to do."

Campbell nodded slightly. "We'll be around town most of the day. I'll look you up later."

"I most likely won't be back until late tonight or tomorrow. Got to ride down to the Indian reservation."

Campbell's eyes turned shrewd. "If it's about work, they don't hire except through government lists."

"It's not about work, Mister Campbell, it's about a little boy."

Campbell turned that over in his mind before saying. "Indian child?"

"No, but the marshal got a piece of paper

sayin' I got to hand this little boy over to Mister Beale."

Campbell looked thoughtful. "Frank Beale's got nothing to do with little kids, or even big ones, if they aren't redskins. . . . I don't understand this."

Joe looked at the pair of rangemen sitting patiently out in sunlight, then back to their employer. "It's a long story and if I don't strike out soon I won't even get down there until evening." He would have moved past but Marshal Glover came strolling northward from the direction of his office. He nodded to both men but looked longest at Joe Bryan. "I been waiting," he said quietly.

Joe squinted a little. "I was on my way down to see you. . . . I'm not going to hand Wes over to you, I'm going down to the reservation and hunt up Mister Beale."

Glover was expressionless. "Goin' to take the little boy with you?"

"No."

Glover's jaw muscles rippled but before he could speak James Campbell said, "What is this about, Henry?"

Glover turned his attention away from Joe and said, "Come on down to the office, both of you. Jim, I got a damned federal order from Beale about a little Indian kid this gent came to town with."

Campbell scowled. "He just told me the kid isn't Indian, Henry."

Glover's color mounted. He glanced around then said, "All I can tell you is that I got this damned order from Frank Beale. You want to see it?"

Campbell turned toward his waiting riders. "Put up the horses with Hickson, then go on up to the saloon. I'll be along directly."

Marshal Glover led the way, erect and unsmiling. He had not expected this kind of a complication. It only added to the personal discomfort he felt about the whole affair. He was not endowed by nature with a willingness to pursue or apprehend small children.

At the office he handed James Campbell the legal order, then went to the stove for a cup of coffee as the cowman read. When he turned, legs wide in front of the stove, he tasted the coffee and waited.

This was none of Campbell's business. On the other hand, James Campbell was a wealthy stockman, the largest landowner in the area. If he decided to buy into someone's problem, he could be just about overwhelming. He had that kind of a reputation.

The older man put the paper gently back atop the desk and gazed thoughtfully at Marshal Glover. It looked to Joe Bryan as though Glover were bracing himself. Campbell then turned to Joe with a question. "Where is this child? I'd like to see him."

"Up at my sister's house," Joe replied.

Glover interrupted. "His sister is Wes Turner's widow."

Campbell looked surprised but said nothing for a moment or two, then he smiled slightly at the lawman. "Is there anything about that order that's got to be done right now, Henry?"

"Well, Beale will know I got it, Jim. He'll expect some kind of action on my part right soon." Glover put down his cup and went back to his desk. "Maybe not today, but sure as hell tomorrow or the next day."

Campbell nodded and turned toward the door. "Tomorrow, Henry." After he and Joe left, Marshal Glover leaned far back in a chair and rolled his eyes ceilingward. "Tomorrow," he said aloud. "Tomorrow with Jim Campbell is any damned day he wants to make it." He rocked forward and glared at the legal order. "I'd give a pint of good whiskey to know what son-of-a-bitch went and told Frank Beale about that little kid!"

A huge old faded gray freight outfit ground past in the roadway out in front of the marshal's office, drawn by eight good-quality mules. The swamper was sitting erect on the high seat taking in the sights of the town, the driver at his side was big and thick and bearded. His checkered flannel shirt was faded and dirty.

Marshal Glover stared, then arose with an oath. There had been a town ordinance against freight outfits using Main Street for five years. Freighters either went around town or they squeezed down the back alleys to unload. He grabbed his hat and slammed out of the offce to roar at the freighter, who turned to look back without pulling on his lines. What he saw was a man even larger than he was, wearing a badge, and red in the face as he started after the wagon. The freighter hauled down to a halt, which made saddle-horse, rig and wagon traffic either squeeze around it or halt stone-still because there was not enough room.

Henry Glover went up the side of the huge old wagon, stepping from the roadway to the forewheel hub, to a worn-smooth steel side-board stirrup, and grabbed the seat railing as he came face to face with a frightened swamper and a dark-eyed, uncertain big rig-owner.

He leaned past the swamper and said,

"What the hell do you think you're doing? There's a town ordinance against outfits this size using Main Street."

The powerfully built bearded man let slack lines slide through his hands as he studied the furious lawman. "I didn't see no sign," he grumbled.

"You don't have to see no sign, you damned idiot. There's not a town within a thousand miles where a rig this big can go down the main roadway!" Henry's nostrils were flared, his eyes were fiery. The swamper, who was young and wiry and small, shrank as far back as he could. The driver's tongue made a darting circuit of his lips before he said, "All right, Marshal. All right. I just didn't know is all. All right. We'll pull on through and set up camp outside town. Only I got freight for the general store."

Glover's fury was burning out. "There is an alley on the east side of town. The general store's got a loading platform out back. Mister, if you ever do this again I'll lock you up for six months just on general principles. You understand me?"

The big bearded man smiled feebly. "Yes, sir, Marshal." Then he watched Glover climb back down to the roadway before whistling up his mules. His swamper looked over at the freighter. "He was mad, Mister Smith."

The bearded man nodded. "Yes sir, he was for a fact, Jim. Mostly though, I knew they didn't allow it here but I didn't know the damned town marshal was that big and mean. He looked like he might shoot a man, Jim. . . . We'll set up camp then walk back an see if that alleyway is wide enough. . . . Yes sir, he was mad for a damned fact, only it don't seem likely a person would get *that* mad over one freight wagon comin' through their town. I'd say somethin' else was botherin' that man, Jim."

CHAPTER 14

Joe's Observations

Mary acknowledged Joe's introduction of James Campbell. Wes was eating at the kitchen table and slid down to run toward Joe. Joe leaned down and they shook hands, then Wes laughed. He was introduced to Mister Campbell and there was an instantaneous change. He became still, silent and expressionless. Campbell smiled, gravely shook hands, then straightened up studying the child. Mary told him to go finish his dinner and the child returned to the kitchen without a backward glance. Mary looked at her brother. "Do you remember we worried that he couldn't talk?"

Joe remembered very well.

"Well . . . I heard him out in the backyard scolding a tan dog that was out in the alley — in Spanish."

Joe thought about that, then said, "His father was a trader somewhere down along the border. A white man, but he'd speak

Spanish, Mary."

Campbell agreed. "They got to, ma'am. There is more Spanish spoken down there than English." Campbell looked steadily at Mary Jane. He only looked elsewhere when Joe said, "I'd guess you know more about Indians than I do, Mister Campbell."

The old cowman was holding his hat in his hands when he said, "He's maybe a third Indian. No more'n that." His gaze drifted back to Mary. "You got a good motherin' instinct, Miz Turner."

She reddened and turned as she said, "Dinner? I'll have it ready in ten minutes. As soon as I've washed Wes and turned him loose to go back out and work on his fort." She held out her hand and James Campbell gave her his hat without taking his eyes off her face. She smiled at her brother. "Sit in here if you'd like. I'll call you."

Joe turned toward a chair but the old cowman watched Mary Jane out of sight before doing the same. Then, as he sat down, he became brisk. "Beale's been told wrong, Joe. That's a 'breed child, it's not a full-blood. In fact if I hadn't spent fifty years in this country where they got every shade of color from black-brown to pink-white, mostly in between, I'd think the boy might be part Mex, but the features aren't right for that. He's part Indian, but not a hell of a lot. . . .

"I've seen your sister before, now an' then in town, but I don't get in very often. I knew her husband to nod to. It's a real pity she came up widowed."

Joe was relaxing in a chair watching the cowman's face. He said, "I didn't know about Conley until we got back yesterday. You could have said something."

Campbell settled back in his chair. "I didn't feel like talkin' about that, or much of anything else yestiddy. Al'd been with me since he was pretty young. Somebody works for you that long and keeps your interests at heart, you get fond of him."

Joe nodded solemnly.

Campbell cleared his throat and peering over his shoulder in the direction of the kitchen, then faced back and spoke in a lowered voice. "Your sister's a fine-lookin' woman. I noticed that some years back, but like I said, I don't get to town very often."

Joe said nothing and gazed at the older man until Campbell reddened, cleared his throat again and became brisk. "Well now — let Frank Beale come up here. It's his darned paper, not yours. Let him ride his rear sore, an' when he gets up here show him the child.

Frank's been around Indians long enough to know a full-blood when he sees one."

Joe speculated about this advice and for some reason had a misgiving. "I'd like to know the law about this thing, Mister Campbell."

The cowman waved that away when he said, "I expect you would, but that's Frank's job. He's the one that's got to prove . . . " He lowered his voice again, this time looking keenly at the younger man. "It's none of my concern, Joe, but how come you to have this little boy?"

Joe understood exactly what the older man was thinking. "He's not a catch-colt, Mister Campbell," he replied, and launched into a full explanation of his encounter with the old Hawk at a place called Spirit Meadow, and although Campbell did not interrupt, his expression and his eyes became lively the longer he listened. Whe Joe had finished, Campbell leaned back looking pensive.

He said, "Hawk. Describe him, Joe."

Joe complied and before he had finished, Campbell was bleakly grinning. "Hawk's not his name. At least it's not his borned-name. You just described a white man I knew thirty, forty years ago. I thought sure he was dead by now. His name is Aaron Love. He lived with the Indians, hunted and even made war with 'em. In my day they called men like old Love squawmen or renegades. Hell, Aaron must be eighty."

Joe conceded that Hawk was old, but that was not what he remembered most about the man. "He planned that whole thing, right from when he shot that old sow bear in the rear with an arrow to waitin' until I was asleep to fetch the little boy to camp, then riding away. I'll bet money he planned it like that."

James Campbell bobbed his head. "I could tell you stories about Aaron Love until the cows came home, and mostly they'd be about someone sly as a fox and as hard to find. Even back then, when the army'd have given a man twenty good horses just to lead them to his hideouts, he was more shadow than man."

Joe nodded. "Someday, maybe, Mister Campbell. Right now — "

"Right now it's the child. What did you have in mind for him?"

"Bringing his down here, gettin' him fed right, put some decent clothes on him, then find him a home." Joe sighed. "I made a bad mistake, Mister Campbell." Joe flicked a glance in the direction of the kitchen. "I never should have brought him here. My sister has no children. I never even thought she'd latch onto the boy like she has. I haven't seen her in years, but I can tell you that in just a few days she's become as protective as a bear with a cub. She changed right in front of my eyes, an' in just a few days."

Campbell was going to speak when Mary Jane came to the parlor door to tell them dinner was ready.

Before sitting down, Campbell went to the rear door to watch the little boy at work on his project of slats and tufts of grass. When he returned he smiled at Mary Jane and she smiled back. Then he said, "He settled in like a puppy, didn't he?"

Mary Jane smiled again, more openly this time, then served up their meal. During it she told them stories about the child: how quickly he learned things, how good-natured he was. When she paused for breath Joe looked at James Campbell and got back an almost imperceptible nod of the older man's head. Joe's suspicion was confirmed about his sister's sudden, almost fierce, interest in the child.

After they had eaten and after James Campbell had thanked Mary Jane for her hospitality and had praised her cooking, the men left the house. Out front, as the old cowman was putting on his hat, he squinted in the direction of the saloon and said, "Jack an' Jim must have figured I fell down and died somewhere. You care for a drink now, Joe?"

Joe shrugged. It was still too early but Campbell had won his respect. As they crossed the road Campbell said, "I'll tell Henry Glover to send that paper back to Frank Beale. Then we'll see what he wants to do about it." As they entered the saloon he continued, "I know Frank pretty well. Knew him when he tried to hire on around the country as a rider. Hell, he couldn't even saddle a horse right, let alone pull a calf or shoe a horse. So naturally, he ended up workin' for the government."

Kincaid and Hudson were playing blackjack at a distant table looking relaxed but bored. They came over to join Joe and Campbell at the bar. Neither of the cowboys seemed to be carrying a grudge.

Later in the afternoon when Joe went down to look in on his horse, he encountered Marshall Glover. The lawman eyed him warily. He'd had a long discussion with James Campbell before the old cowman and his riders left town. Glover and the fat man named Hickson who owned the livery barn had been talking, but as Joe walked toward them Hickson went hurriedly out back where his corrals were.

Glover came right to the point. "Y'know,

old Jim's forgot more about Indians than you an' I'll ever know. He said your little boy's at best no more'n a third redskin."

Joe looked around for his sorrel horse. It was standing hipshot and dozing in a cool stall with fresh bedding under it. Glover followed him over to the stall to lean on the door looking in. "Good animal," he murmured. "I liked him down yonder yesterday." Still looking at the horse he went on, "I'll send the paper back to Beale in the morning, He's goin' to be mad as a wet hen."

"Why? Because you didn't lock up the little boy?"

"No. Because I wrote across the front of his paper that your little boy's not an Indian." Glover continued to study the sorrel horse. "What do you think of Mister Campbell now?"

"He's different from how he was yesterday. Maybe it's like you said, losing his tophand hit him pretty hard."

Henry Glover continued to lean on the stall door. "You wouldn't expect him to come into town two days in a row if you knew him. He had something else on his mind when he came in today."

Joe eyed the big, burly lawman but said nothing.

Glover finally turned away from the horse. "He made that long ride to hire you on again."

Joe thought that over. "He didn't say a word about anything like that, Marshal."

Glover's brown eyes glinted. "He will, when he figures the time is ripe. You'll get to know him if you stay around. He's tough as rawhide, rough when he don't like the way things are going, and they say he's mean to boot. But I've never found him to be mean — he's just naturally hard as nails. There's one thing about those old-timers you want to remember though: they're sly. They don't give up an' they scheme a lot." Glover straightened up off the stall door, his eyes fixed on Joe Bryan. "I'm hungry. See you around town. I'll mail off Beale's letter in the morning. By day after tomorrow you can expect to hear from him. If there's one thing about Frank Beale, it's that he don't like for someone to yank the chair out from under him."

After Marshal Glover had gone, the wispy little old watery-eyed nightman came along with a three-tined feedfork. He smiled at Joe and paused to look in at the sorrel horse. "How does he look to you?"

"Fine. Rested up an' fed an' cuffed."

"Well, it took me considerable time. When

folks come through and like the way I look after their animals so well, they show real appreciation."

Joe looked into the thin, lined old face and dug in his pocket for a silver coin which he handed to the older man. The hostler beamed broadly and went away with a new spring in his step.

The fat man came up from the rear of the barn and halted to glare. "I saw you give him money," he said. "You know what that means, cowboy?"

Joe nodded. "Yeah. It means I appreciate him looking after my horse, currying him and all."

The fat man's eyes widened, his color climbed. "He didn't curry your horse or put fresh beddin' in the stall. Did he tell you that, the confounded runt? I did those things. And I exercised your horse in the round corral this morning. And now you know what'll happen?"

"No. What?"

"He'll be up at the saloon with his snout buried in a mug and when he gets back this evening, *if* he gets back, the old rumpot, I'll have to roll him into the hay and do all his work for him."

Joe gently rubbed the tip of his nose. "I

didn't know he drank, Mister Hickson. . . . I'll tell you something; this darned country has a way of gettin' me into trouble even when I'm standing still and minding my own business."

He turned and left the barn heading toward the roadway, leaving the fat man glowering after him.

The afternoon was advancing, trade seemed to be slackening off, at least the pedestrian and horse traffic was not as heavy as it had been. Joe went back up to his sister's house. She was giving Wes a bath in the kitchen. Joe heard them laughing even before he entered.

Wes looked like a small drowned rat. Mary was flushed and merry-eyed and when she saw her brother in the doorway she rolled her eyes. "I didn't know any child could get as filthy as this one can, rooting out there in the dirt like a shoat. . . . Joe, what about Frank Beale's letter?"

He told her what James Campbell recommended and ended up by confirming he intended to follow Campbell's advice. Mary lifted Wes from the old tub and handed him a towel. She then walked out into the parlor, and when Joe met her there she looked very earnestly up at him. "Don't let them take him away," she said. "Please?"

He smiled at her. "No one's goin' to take him away from you, Mary. . . . I just wonder if you've figured all this out. He's a little boy, Mary. You'll be lettin' youself in for a long haul."

She knew something about young boys. She had watched them with a wistful longing for years. It wasn't the hazards or the tribulations that troubled her. "Suppose that man you called Hawk should come around? It's his grandson."

Joe thought of something that had puzzled him from the beginning: why had old Hawk stolen the child in the first place? He certainly knew he would be unable to care for the child. Joe did not even believe old Hawk wanted the child. He was not the kind of an individual who would wish to change his way of living to accommodate a small boy. Not after living his free kind of life for more than half a century.

"Joe . . . ?"

He brought his attention back to his sister. "I doubt that he'll ever show up. Mister Campbell knew him forty years ago. He said Hawk's about eighty years old by now. But if he does come around, I'll talk to him, Mary."

"He could go to the law."

Joe smiled at her. "I don't think he'd even think about doing that. Mary, unless I sure am off course, he gave me the child because he figured me out as someone who'd find him a decent home. I think he didn't want the child himself — for some reason he didn't want his dead daughter's child to be left with his father either — likely we'll never know Hawk's reason for taking the boy. I don't think you have much to worry about on that score."

"Well, but what about Frank Beale?"

He eyed her for a moment in silence then he said, "Mary, did you ever talk to James Campbell before today?"

"No, why?"

"I just wondered. Anyway, he told the marshal to send that paper back to the reservation. Whatever this Frank Beale figures to do next, I have a feelin' he might end up wishin' he hadn't even thought of it. I wouldn't want Mister Campbell as an enemy. I'd say he's takin' an interest in Wes — and you."

Mary Jane's very blue eyes grew still on her brother's face. "Me, Joe . . . ?"

He nodded slightly. "I'm forty. And I didn't come down in the last rain. I haven't been around women very much but I've sure been around a lot of men. Now I think

I'll go over to the saloon and have a glass of beer."

He left her looking after him as he went back out into the waning hot afternoon.

CHAPTER 15

A Crisis

The reaction of the Indian agent, when he had received his letter back with Marshal Glover's cryptic message scribbled across it, was quick and angry. The marshal had thought there would be no reaction for three or four days. He was wrong. Frank Beale was waiting out front of the jailhouse the same day he received the letter. He was accompanied by three unsmiling, nondescript individuals who had belt guns, which was common, and booted Winchesters, which was a lot less common.

Frank Beale was medium-sized with a slightly hooked nose, a pair of slatey eyes, a deep and lasting tan, and a hint of gray above the ears. He was not a physical match for Marshal Glover, neither were his three expressionless companions; but the moment Henry Glover left the café after breakfast heading for his office and saw those four men waiting for him, he got a knot behind his belt. Frank Beale was quick, venomous, knowledgeable and imbued with an idea of self-importance.

As for the men with him, Glover, after looking them over, recognized them for what they were and discarded any idea of them as opponents. When he stepped up onto the plankwalk fishing for his jailhouse key, he said, "Good morning, gents. I'll fire up the stove and put the coffee on, but maybe we'd better put off talkin' until after the caféman's come an' gone. He's going to bring over some food for my prisoners."

Glover swung the door inward and waved the visitors in first. He went to the stove and kept up a running conversation as he shoved in kindling, got it lighted, then set the damper wide open as he eased in some large pieces of wood. The last thing he did was place his dented old speckled-ware coffeepot atop the stove.

The caféman came barging in laden with little buckets. The smaller ones contained black coffee. The larger ones contained stew made of leftovers.

Glover accompanied him down into the cells, and returned with him. The caféman eyed the four unsmiling men askance, barely nodded and departed.

The stove was popping. Glover filled four

cups with hot coffee from the pot, passed them around, then went to his old chair behind the untidy table and looked straight at Beale.

The Indian agent pulled a folded paper from his pocket and pitched it over atop the table. Glover glanced at it and nodded his head. "That's what I wrote. What about it?"

Beale's retort was brusque. "My information is that the child is a catch-colt out of a reservation woman."

Glover leaned forward. He knew Beale well. He also knew that arguing with him would be the same as arguing with a stone wall, so he said, "You want to see him?"

Beale nodded. "That's why we rode over here, Henry."

Glover's amiable look congealed as he ran a slow glance over Beale's companions. "Who are those gents?" he asked.

"We're having trouble organizing Indian police for the reservation so I got permission from the Department to have these men sworn in until we can get the Indians to police themselves."

Henry Glover nodded as he ran another slow look over the three strangers. The Springville marshal shared a common characteristic among lawmen: he saw red when other peace officers barged into his territory. He brought his gaze back to the Indian agent. "You don't need 'em, Frank. But if you did, someone sworn in by you to police a reservation wouldn't have no more authority in my county than the man in the moon."

The three lean, leathery strangers were looking stonily at Marshal Glover. One thing about all three of them seemed clear: they would be very hard to intimidate.

Frank Beale's answer was short. "They're not here as lawmen. They just rode along with me."

Glover looked sardonic as he said, "Sure they did." He arose."Wait here. I'll go get the little boy."

Beale was on his feet in seconds. "We'll go with you. Where is he?"

"Up the road, stayin' with the sister of the man who brought him to town."

"I see. Well, we'll go with — "

"No, you won't, Frank. You can get some breakfast at the café or you can wait here, but you're not coming with me." As he said this, Marshal Glover came from behind his table, hooked both thumbs in his shellbelt and faced the four men along the office's front wall. He was almost as large as any two of them combined, and right now he did not look like someone who intended to argue.

Beale stood his ground, but only briefly. Then his eyes shifted — and Henry Glover smiled at him. "I figured you'd be sensible, Frank," he said, and started toward the door. One of the reservation policeman was in the way and Henry smiled at him too. The man shuffled out of the way.

Glover was in the open doorway when Beale stopped him. "Nothing clever, Henry."

The marshal's smile widened. "Nothin' clever. It'll only take a few minutes; you boys get comfortable. Help yourselves to more coffee. The child's up at the Widow Turner's place. I'll be right back."

Beale's eyes widened. "Mary Jane Turner — she's got the child?"

"Yes. It was her brother who came to town with him. He's stayin' with his sister too."

"Wait a minute, Henry," Beale said, brows lowering slightly. "This catch-colt is out of Mary Jane's brother?"

Marshal Glover's smile faded. For a couple of moments he regarded the Indian agent without answering, then he said, "Just in case this feller comes back with me — his name is Joe Bryan — I'll give you some advice: Be careful about usin' the term 'catch-colt.' " Glover nodded curtly and closed the door after himself. He was mad all the way through.

The morning was still refreshingly cool. Springville was alive with people who seemed to want to transact their business before the heat arrived. Marshal Glover did not even see the burly, bearded freighter and his wispy youthful swamper until they were less than twenty feet apart, then it registered in his mind who the man was. He started past with a wooden stare and a short nod.

The freighter stopped. He was chewing a toothpick. He had eaten at the café a short while before and was now returning from the harness shop where he'd left a leather trace to be sewn. He said, "Good morning, Marshal," without sounding the least bit sincere. His dark eyes were fixed on Glover in a speculative way. "We done like you said, Marshal. We set up camp south of town in a stand of trees. You got a nice town here. I never been in Springville before." The burly man spat out his toothpick, dark eyes unblinking. "Y'know, last night when I was eatin' supper I got to thinkin' about the way you come up over the side of my wagon and all."

The freighter had just made his second mistake in twenty-four hours. This time Marshal Glover was even angrier than he had been yesterday morning. He returned the bearded man's unfriendly look.

"And you didn't like it," Glover said.

The freighter shuffled until both feet were squarely under his thick body. "No sir, I didn't like it. But I don't carry a gun."

Glover glanced at the slight youth. He was white to the hairline in spite of a suntan, his eyes perfectly round as he looked up at the marshal.

"Might be a good idea to carry one," Henry told the burly man, raising his eyes, "If you're goin' to challenge folks but don't worry about me carryin' one. That goes with my job — like this does too." Henry hit the freighter over the heart with a ham-sized fist. The burly man staggered and grunted but did not fall. Henry followed up his first strike with another one, along the slant of the bearded man's jaw. This time the freighter fell and rolled half off the plankwalk, his filthy shapeless old hat landing farther out in the dust.

Glover looked down as he worked the fingers and knuckles of his right hand. The burly man had a jawbone of solid stone. He turned and said, "Boy, get a bucket of water and dump it over him, an' when he comes around tell him if he wants to take this up, next time to wear his gun."

The swamper was shaking. "Yes sir," he

whispered. "He ain't dead, is he? — there's blood on his mouth."

Henry continued his walk in the direction of the Turner house.

Over in front of the mercantile store several people stood as motionless as statues until the clerk with the black cotton sleeve-protectors came out and said, "Likely he could use some whiskey if one of you folks want to go over and pour it down him."

The little crowd dispersed.

A lanky, hard-faced man had been standing halfway exposed in the jailhouse door watching Marshal Glover walk northward. He stepped back inside and said, "Mister Beale, he just tangled with a dirty-lookin' big feller up the way apiece and knocked him senseless. Are you sure what you said about this place is right?"

"What did I say?" snapped the Indian agent.

"When you told us to get saddled up this morning, you said we was goin' over here to catch an Indian kid and fetch him back, and no one in Springville would try to stop us."

Frank Beale shouldered irritably past and leaned to look northward out the doorway. There were several people trying to prop up a water-soaked, bearded man and a wiry, ragged-looking youth was standing with an empty waterbucket in his hand watching.

Later Joe and Mary Jane were reminiscing over coffee at the kitchen table when Marshal Glover rolled an angry fist over the parlor door. Mary Jane sprang up and left the kitchen. Joe went after another cup of coffee, and as he passed the rear doorway he leaned briefly to watch Wes busy as a beaver out there in brilliant sunlight working on his slat-board and sod structure. Joe grinned to himself. Whatever else Wes might do in life, he seemed to have one attribute that might help him: He perservered. He had been working on that fort, or whatever it was, for four days now. What little Joe recalled about children from seeing them occasionally was that their interest in things did not seem to last more than an hour or two.

He went back to his chair as Mary Jane brought Marshal Glover into the kitchen, then silently went to the stove for another cup of coffee.

Joe nodded and Marshal Glover spat it out: "Beale is down in my office with three reservation policemen that look to me like he found them out behind a saloon somewhere and drug them home to sober them up."

Joe and Mary stared. She said, "Today?"

Glover accepted the cup with his left hand. He had the right one in his lap out of sight where he could open and close it without being observed. The knuckles were swelling.

"He's down there," Glover reiterated and drank the coffee. It did not help his mood any but it was fresh and he was not accustomed to fresh coffee.

Joe sat a moment in thought then arose to go for his hat. As Marshal Glover also arose and thanked Mary Jane for the coffee, she caught his sleeve. "I don't want him up here, Marshal." He saw the look in her eyes and patted her hand, then walked out through the parlor to join Joe. They left the house together. At the gate Glover said, "One of us better get the little boy," and at the look on Joe's face, Marshal Glover wagged his head. "It's got to be done this way. But I'll tell you one thing — when they leave, the kid won't be with them. . . . I think you can do this better than I can. I'll wait out here."

Joe looked back toward the house. After a moment he said, "Marshal, my sister's going to have a fit."

Glover nodded gloomily. "Tell her we'll fetch him back. All I want is for Beale to see the lad. If he knows Indians, he'll know on sight that little boy is not a full-blood."

Joe shifted from one foot to the other. Henry Glover was no help. When their eyes met Henry said, "I'll be down at the jailhouse waiting." He stalked past the little gate on his way southward.

Joe watched Glover's retreating figure until the door up front opened and Mary Jane said, "Joe, what is it?"

He walked heavily toward her, and on the porch told her he had to take Wes down to the jailhouse with him. She reached with one hand to grasp the door staring at him. "No you can't," she said, all three words run together.

"Mary, I'll bring him back. Glover just wants Beale to see the boy, that's all. He's not a reservation Indian. Beale will know that the minute he looks at him."

She was holding the door with both hands when she replied. "Joe . . . no. He will take him."

"Naw. Mary, he's got to see for himself that — "

"There's something I didn't tell you about Frank Beale. He — brought me those flowers and things."

"You told me that."

"He said he'd help me with money. . . . All I had to do was be home when he came up to

Springville. . . . I told him he had a wife. . . . He got mad. . . . I told him if he ever pushed his way into my house again I'd get the pistol and shoot him."

Joe said nothing for a long while. He turned, glanced around, then turned back. "Go get Wes, Mary."

"Joe, please. . . ."

"Get him. I'll have him back here within an hour. . . . Beale . . . well, just don't think about Beale. He's not going to do anything, but if he tries to . . . Mary, fetch Wes, will you please?"

They looked steadily at each other for a small eternity, then she turned and went back through the house, and Joe stepped to the edge of the porch to squint unseeingly at the very distant and heat-blurred mountains.

CHAPTER 16

The Jailhouse Office

Halfway down to the jailhouse there was mud at the side of the plankwalk and the scuffed old planks were also dark with it as Joe held his pace to the stride of the much shorter legs of the child clinging to his hand.

Wes was being brave. Mary Jane's hug and teary eyes had alerted him to trouble, and when Joe had offered his hand, Wes had taken it looking straight up. Joe was not smiling. In fact he looked forbidding to the child. Wes had learned quite a bit about grown people over the last few weeks and like most small animals he instinctively knew not to open his mouth. He looked down at the brass toe-caps, not even noticing the water-darkened duckboards as he walked across them.

The only time he looked up was when Joe stopped in front of the jailhouse. He had never seen such a building before.

Joe glanced downward, saw the grave look,

the noncommittal wide eyes, and squeezed Wes's fingers. He smiled. "This won't take long, and you'll be back workin' on your fort."

Joe opened the door and, with the child still clutching his hand, walked into the jailhouse office where five men turned in stony silence to look at him. He increased his grip on Joe.

Marshal Glover put down a cup of coffee he had been holding, winked at the child and motioned Joe toward a bench on the north side of the room. He led Wes over and sat down with him.

Joe knew one man in the room, Marshal Glover. He studied the three lean, hard-looking men, then fixed his attention upon the man he thought would be Frank Beale. Henry Glover also ignored the three reservation policemen and introduced Frank Beale to Joe. Neither man offered his hand. Beale was more interested in the little boy, but Joe was decidedly interested in Beale.

Henry Glover, standing behind his table, leaned on it and said, "Frank . . .?"

Beale did not reply, he was still staring at the child. Once he glanced at Joe, then down at the child again — and color began climbing into his face.

The marshal spoke again. "Is that a reservation Indian, Frank?"

Beale ignored the question. He looked furious but did not speak for a long time. Not until Glover addressed him again. "Cat got your tongue? You wanted proof, there it is. That boy's no more a reservation Indian than I am."

Beale stiffened. "Then we better take both of you back with us," he said.

Glover stared. Joe Bryan's grip on the child's hand tightened. The marshal straightened back off his table. "What the hell are you talking about, Frank? Look at that boy. He's no more'n maybe a third Indian."

Beale's stare at Glover was cold and unwavering. "We got Indians on the reservation just as light colored."

Joe spoke for the first time since entering the office. "With features like his, Mister Beale?"

The Indian agent turned and snapped his answer. "Yes. We can run in two dozen women who could be this child's mother." His slate-gray eyes were fixed on Joe Bryan. "Catch-colts out of reservation squaws count as Indians."

Joe's expression did not change but he met the other man's eyes with an icy stare. "He's not a catch-colt, Mister Beale, but if he was,

I'll be damned if I can see you takin' him to a reservation."

Beale's retort was short and infuriating. "You don't know the law, Mister Bryan. If he's not a catch-colt, then tell me what he is?"

"His mother was half-Indian. His father is a white man who trades out of a wagon down along the Mex line somewhere. His mother died a few weeks back."

"I see. And his father died too?"

Joe's hand was sweaty in Wes's grip. "I don't know anything about his father."

"How did you get him, Mister Bryan?"

"From his grandfather, an old man called Hawk. I met Hawk in the mountains north of here at a place called Spirit Meadow. . . . He left the little boy with me."

Beale glanced over to where his three reservation policemen were standing near the gun-rack. His lips widened in a faint sneer. "What would you say, gents — Indian or not Indian?"

One of the policemen paused as he chewed his cud of tobacco and answered quietly and gruffly. "Indian, Mister Beale." The other two men nodded gravely, looking squarely at the man they had ridden to Springville with.

Beale ignored Joe and Wes to face Marshal Glover. "I got a warrant in my pocket, Henry.

You want to see it?"

Glover stared. So did Joe Bryan. It was finished; Beale had said the little boy was a reservation Indian and that was the end of it.

Joe looked at the Indian agent in disbelief. Turning to meet the stare, Beale was still flushed and his slatey eyes were bleak. "Do you really think anyone is going to believe some old man came to your camp in the mountains and rode off after giving you his grandson? Mister Bryan, you had plenty of time to make up a more believable story than that one."

Joe freed his right hand and leaned to arise. From one of the men near the gunrack a cold voice said, "Just set back, mister." The reservation policeman holding the gun cocked it.

Henry Glover turned half toward the wall. The same lanky, cold-eyed policeman swung his cocked gun toward the marshal. "Don't do nothin' rash," he warned.

Beale waited until there was no more movement, then blew out a big sighing breath. "Henry, if you'd done your job we wouldn't have had to make the ride up here, mostly in the dark and cold this morning."

Glover turned his head. "You don't know what you're doing," he told the Indian agent. "The sky is going to fall on you. That's no

Indian kid and you know it."

Beale did not yield. "I told you — I can round up two dozen squaws as light as that boy." He paused a moment, still looking at the town marshal. "Prove to me he's not an Indian pup out of some squaw an' a white man. Prove it, Henry, and I'll walk out of here an' you folks can keep him."

Joe had not taken his eyes off Beale since the reservation policeman had cocked his handgun. "All right," he said quietly. I'll prove it to you."

"How?" Beale snapped.

"We'll go up into Spirit Meadow country and hunt down his grandfather."

Beale's expression mirrored disgust. "Cowboy, I've been in those mountains. It would take a day just to get up there. Then it'd take a lot longer to try and find someone I don't believe exists — and that would take more time than I'm going to spend on this matter. What would happen to the little boy while we were riding around in circles in the mountains? He'd disappear, wouldn't he?" Beale started to turn away in contempt.

Joe brought him back around. "I'm trying to give you proof, Mister Beale. You don't figure to give me a chance because your mind's made up. I told you the truth about his grandfather." Joe waited a long time for the Indian agent's reply and did not get it.

Beale opened his mouth to speak angrily, then checked himself. He turned toward Henry Glover again. "We'll take the boy with us. I've got the authority to do it and you know that, Henry. We don't have to prove anything; you and Bryan have to."

The man holding the cocked six-gun shuffled his feet as he repositioned himself. His companions along the wall did not move. One of them seemed scarcely to be breathing.

Beale said more. "Henry, you're a peace officer. Your job is to support the law."

"Don't tell me my job, Frank!" exclaimed the marshal.

"All right, I won't," Beale retorted, and slowly fished inside his coat and brought forth a folded sheet of paper which he dropped atop the other papers on Glover's desk. "That's the federal warrant. It's signed by the Territorial attorney. I never knew you to take sides before, Henry, and you shouldn't have done it this time. You can't wear a badge and buck the law at the same time."

Joe thought Marshal Glover was going to come across his table at the Indian agent, and he might have if that man with the cocked gun hadn't gruffly said, "Steady, Marshal. I'll cut you in two."

Glover's jaw muscles rippled, his big hands were knotted. Joe stared intently at the Indian agent. He did not seem to be carrying a gun, at least there was no bulge beneath the coat, and he probably knew that Marshal Glover was a bad man to cross, but he was looking Glover in the eye and defying him.

Joe felt a spasm in the little hand he was holding and looked down. Wes was white as a sheet and biting his lower lip. Joe raised his arm to put it around the child's shoulders. When Beale turned slowly away from Glover and met Joe's stare he said, "We brought an extra horse. You just sit there." Beale then jerked his head at the man near the gunrack who had seemed petrified. "Bring the horses up here, Curly."

The policeman went out of the office very fast. Joe did not take his eyes off the Indian agent as he said, "You don't take him." Beale turned to face him. Joe gently shook his head. "You're going to get yourself killed."

Beale stared.

Joe nodded toward the man with the cocked gun. "You'll get off one shot. I'll get off the next one — right through you, mister."

The gruff man holding the six-gun sneered. "You won't get off nothin', cowboy, because

I'll blow your head off."

Joe looked at Marshal Glover, and the lawman said to the man holding the six-gun, "You know I'll have a bullet in you before you finish pulling the trigger." Then Glover looked at the other resevation policeman who seemed to want no part in this fight.

The man with the gun did not reply, but glanced from Glover to the Indian agent. Beale took his cue exactly as Henry Glover had. But his response was different. "Henry . . . do you know what you're doing?"

Glover did not answer, he reached up with his left hand, freed the badge on his shirt and dropped it atop the desk. Then he said, "Yeah, I know what I'm doing. I'm going to kill that man in self-defense just like any citizen has the right to do."

Beale paled, his tongue nervously darting across his lips. He looked over at Joe Bryan whose eyes had never left him. "You are both crazy. I can be back here in two days with soldiers. I can get two more warrants, one for each of you. Do you want to fight the army — over one catch-colt?"

Joe addressed the man holding the gun. "Put it up or use it — and if you use it, you and your friend here, and maybe the marshal or I'll go out with you — but you sure as hell won't be around to see it. *Put it up!*"

The silence was so deep there was no room for sound. Joe disengaged his arm from Wes's shoulders and leaned forward on the bench to free the holster on his right side. He was watching the man with the gun. Beale lost his color, then finally said, "Put it up. We'll come back with the army." The man eased off the hammer and leathered his weapon; the tension snapped, leaving everyone in the room feeling limp.

Marshal Glover gestured. "Out, Frank."

Beale stood his ground briefly, then went to the door and held it open for his policemen to leave first. He stood a long time staring at Marshal Glover. "You ruined yourself, Henry," he finally said. "You'll be a fugitive. You not only broke your lawman's pledge to support the law, you threatened a government Indian agent."

Beale went out and closed the door after himself. Marshal Glover dropped down on his chair. He said, "That was close. In fact, that was as close as I ever came."

Joe nodded. "Me too. Would you have shot him?"

Glover nodded his head. "Yes. Unless he shot me first. How about you?"

"Him, yes. But Beale didn't have a gun. At

least I didn't see one."

Glover fished in a lower desk drawer for a bottle of rye whiskey which he uncapped and held out. Joe took two swallows and passed it back. Henry Glover took four swallows. As he was putting the bottle back he said, "I'll be damned if I can even guess how this is goin' to turn out."

"Will he come back with the army?"

"Yes, if he can talk the army into doing it. Frank's a vindictive, pig-headed, conceited horse's rear."

Joe looked down as small fingers crept into his hand. He said, "Come on, Wes, let's go home."

Marshal Glover watched the door close behind them, and leaned with a grunt for his bottom drawer again.

CHAPTER 17

Through Heat-Haze

Joe did not tell his sister the details, he simply led Wes to the back door, patted his shoulders and left him to cross the yard toward his slat-and-mud fort. Then he told her Frank Beale had claimed Wes belonged on the reservation and Mary sat down.

Joe shook the coffeepot, poured two cups full, set one in front of his sister and sat opposite her with the other. He was lost in thought when she said, "I had a bad feeling. Frank has a vicious streak. He's vindictive. The minute he found out the child was with me, he made up his mind to settle his score with me through the little boy."

Joe nodded without speaking. He had difficulty believing that anyone would go to such lengths to avenge being spurned, but Beale did appear to be uncommonly willful and mean.

Mary Jane asked what would happen now, and Joe drained his cup before answering.

"I don't know. It's up to him," Joe smiled. "Marshal Glover's an honest man. He took Wes's part against Beale, which maybe wasn't the smartest thing he's ever done. Lawmen are supposed to enforce the law, not take sides." Joe continued to smile at his sister. "If I wasn't worried about Beale's coming back, I'd ride up into the mountains and hunt that old man down and drag him back here by the scruff of his neck. That's the best solution — that, or saddling up and riding so far off with Wes no one could ever find him."

Mary Jane slowly shook her head. "No, Joe."

He arose, leaned and patted her hand. "I was just talking. I'm goin' over to the saloon to do a little thinking. Be back directly."

Before leaving the kitchen he stepped to the rear door and looked for Wes. He was sitting in the grass, hands lying lifelessly in his lap staring straight ahead. Joe turned. "Mary, he was pretty scairt down there. Maybe what he needs right now is for someone to hold him."

He left, went across the road and onto the far-side plankwalk before someone called his name. Marshal Glover was closing the distance between them with a thrusting stride. He stopped on the sidewalk to say, "You ever get the feelin' you'd ought to be in some other line of work?" Before Bryan could reply, the marshal steered him past the spindle door and across the dark, cool room to the bar. The barman went after a bottle and glasses.

Glover leaned down. "What's got me puzzled is what's behind what Frank did? He knew as well as you and I know, that child is not a reservation Indian, yet there he stood swearing up and down he is. Joe, Frank Beale's been on that job quite a spell. No one could fool him about something like this. He deliberately made a case out against the kid — without one damned jot of sense to it. . . . Why? Frank's not a fool, so why did he try to take the child?"

Their bottle arrived, the barman filled both glasses, then departed. Joe stood looking at the amber whiskey. He had no intention of telling Marshal Glover about Beale and his sister — it would sound too ridiculous even to imply the Indian agent had acted as he had to spite Mary Jane Turner. Even if it turned out to be true.

Glover toyed with his shotglass. He had not really desired the drink, he'd had enough whiskey at his office. He leaned there in solemn thought trying to puzzle through to an explantion of something that had him baffled. After a while he said, "I tried to guess whether he'll really try to get the army to help him or not. . . . If an army officer comes up here and takes one look at the little boy, he'll know for a fact the child is not an Indian. Would Frank really risk being humiliated like that, for Chris'sake?"

Joe only made one remark. "You know him better than I do, Marshal." Joe downed his jolt and as he pushed the little glass away he said, "If the army comes up here with him — what can it do?"

Glover spoke positively when he replied, sounding like someone who had dealt with the army before. "It can do just about anythin' it wants to do. Maybe you didn't know this, but territories are governed by the army. States got civilian lawmen an' administrators. Until this territory becomes a state, the army runs it the way it figures it should be run." Glover paused, then went on. "The army knows Indians pretty well. Unless a blind officer leads the soldiers who might come here, he's goin' to take one look at the little boy and get mad at Frank for claimin' we are refusing to hand over a reservation Indian. That kid don't look any more like a full-blood, or even a half-blood, than I do."

"Maybe Beale won't come back with soldiers, Marshal." Joe felt sure that if Beale had pursued the matter after seeing that the boy was not a full-blooded Indian just to spite Mary, he's had his fun and would cause no more trouble.

Henry Glover knew the Indian agent too well to commit himself. "Maybe not, only don't bet your wages on it." Glover downed his shot and reached to refill both their glasses.

Joe covered his with his palm. "If I didn't think something might happen while I was gone, Marshal, I'd go back into the mountains and hunt down that damned old man if it took me six months to catch him."

Glover didn't cotton to that idea at all. "Six months? Hell, by then the smoke will have cleared. Frank'll do whatever he figures he's got to do within the next few days. Could you find that old man in, say, a couple of days?" When Joe did not reply, Glover studied his face, then grunted. "You couldn't."

Joe's speculations on the topic of Hawk were already going off on a different tangent before the lawman had spoken those last two words. He slapped Glover lightly on the back and said, "I'm goin' for a horseback ride," and walked out of the saloon leaving Henry Glover glowering at himself in the back-bar mirror. Horseback ride? What kind of damned foolishness was that!

Hickson, the overweight liveryman, was out back watching some horses in a corral when Joe Bryan came walking down the alley looking for him. When they met, Hickson pointed to a dapple-gray gelding as though there had never been trouble between them.

"Now there's somethin' a horse trader gets hold of once in a blue moon. Five years old but still dappled, gentle as a lamb, pretty as a picture and well broke." Hickson was not looking at Joe; he was looking at the horse. "I give six dollars for him. Normally I don't tell how much I give because it'd get around an' when I put him up for thirty dollars, no one would pay that much."

Joe settled a boot on the lowest corral log. "Then why tell me?" he asked.

"Because you're not goin' to try an' buy him an' I'm not goin' to sell him." Hickson turned finally. "You want your horse?"

"Yeah. Going to ride out aways."

The fat man turned to lead the way back inside. "Good thing. He's gettin' snuffy in that stall just gettin' exercised in the round corral every two or three days. You still want him to be grained? Because if you don't expect to ride him a lot, the grain'll make him hard to handle."

Joe's reply was about what Hickson wanted. "All right. Just hay."

Joe waited for his sorrel horse to be led out. Red had indeed done very well since his return from the fight down at the boulder field. His hair was shiny and darker, his eyes were bright and willing. Joe did the saddling and bridling with Hickson standing by to watch. As Joe turned to lead the sorrel out into the alley to mount, Hickson said, "He's goin' to try you, mister."

Joe turned the horse three times instead of the customary two times, snugged up the cinch and looked at the fat man across the saddleseat. "He never bucked in his life," he said, and stepped up.

Red's little ears were back. He stood absolutely still. Joe squeezed him and the sorrel horse took two steps, bogged his head and took to his rider like the devil taking to a crippled saint.

Joe lost one stirrup. Hickson was standing back there yelling encouragement, though it was unclear which creature he was encouraging.

Red might not have lost his rider if he had bucked in a straight line, but as Joe was trying to find that flopping stirrup, Red sunfished to the left and Joe left him like a bird. He came down in the alley so hard it half knocked the breath out of him.

Hickson was a horseman. He knew exactly what the sorrel horse would do next, and caught both flying reins as Red tried to run back into the barn.

He led the horse back where Joe was beating dust off with his hat. "Never bucked, eh?"

Joe looked up grinning a little sheepishly. "Yeah. Once." He turned Red again, twice this time, and was rough about it. He toed in and this time cheeked the horse, rose up and came down gently on the saddleseat. Red did not move. Hickson said, "You know what's bothering him?"

Joe knew. "Barn sour. When I get back don't put him in a stall again."

Hickson nodded and leaned against the rear-barn opening to watch as Joe evened up the reins, and instead of squeezing the sorrel again, turned him to the left to get him untracked, then back to the right, and rode him up the alley until he found a wide place and left the alley heading west and slightly northward.

Two miles out he squeezed. This time Red was a perfect gentleman. He broke over into a rocking-chair lope and kept it.

The sun was high. There was increasing

heat, and the usual accompanying hot haze far ahead that seemed to ripple in the still air. Joe let Red get it all out of his system, then hauled the sorrel horse down to a fast walk and held him to that gait until he could distinguish big trees in the distance. He did not make out rooftops until he was much closer.

He was not hopeful of finding James Campbell in the yard at this time of day, but with nothing else to do he was willing to sit in the shade and wait for him to return. There were some things he would like to ponder more about anyway, and Springville, where interruptions were fairly constant, was a poor place to do any kind of thinking. At least that was Joe Bryan's opinion. Along with it went another opinion: Towns were for people who did not know any better than to live all ganged together like prairie dogs.

Approaching from the southwest he saw limp laundry, what seemed to be dish towels, hanging from a lariat rope that had been stretched between two trees. Beyond the laundry was the cookhouse. Opposite that was a large old log barn with unevenly hand-split sugarpine shingles. There was a large log bunkhouse too, with a broad porch out front. Among other outbuildings, Joe recognized a wagon shed, open in front; a smithy, also open in front; a smokehouse; and what looked to be a springhouse which was closer to the main house.

If he'd had doubt about whose yard he rode into it was dispelled by someone's meticulous handiwork with a hot iron. The name CAMPBELL RANCH had been burned on the left side of the front doorless barn opening, and below the name, what Joe read as a Rafter C cattle and horse brand.

There was not a sound, not even the usual barking of a dog. He tied up out front of the barn and looked all around. There was no sign of life of any kind. He entered the barn. The stalls were also empty, but out back in the working corrals of peeled logs, he found five horses standing rump-sprung in tree shade sleeping. They had that same Rafter C mark on their left shoulders, but small, the entire mark no larger than a man's hand.

He strolled back up front. A squatty, overweight man with a mass of coarse dark hair shot through with iron gray was sitting on the porch of the cookhouse. He called from across the yard, "You lookin' for someone, mister?"

Joe crossed over. "Mister Campbell," he said.

The bushy-headed man waved a thick arm. "Him and Gus went thataway right after breakfast. Everyone else went southwest to start the summer gather." The heavy man lowered his arm and stared unabashedly at Joe until he reached a decision, then he said, "Put up your horse out'n the sun, then come on back. I got a cobbler I never made before an' need someone to try it on." The cook grinned and Joe grinned back, then went to care for the sorrel horse. He stalled him in the barn because he was too sweaty to be turned out under direct sunlight, then he returned to the cookhouse and the squatty man had already put a big bowl of peach cobbler on the long dinner table. Joe dumped his hat and picked up the spoon as he said, "Joe Bryan."

"Manuel Lewis," the cook replied. "Taste it. I never tried anythin' that fancy before, I seen the recipe in an old magazine someone threw out of the bunkhouse."

Except that the cobbler was more nearly soup than dessert, it was very good, and Joe said so. Manuel Lewis looked more relieved than pleased as he sat down opposite. With a directness that *cocineros* could get away with but rangeriders could not, he asked a direct question. "You lookin' for work?"

Joe nodded his head and went right on eating. He had not been aware of hunger until he had started on the cobbler. Manuel Lewis watched him eat; there was no better compliment a cook could be paid, usually anyway.

Lewis leaned on the table. "You know Mister Campbell?"

Joe nodded again as he tipped up the bowl to use his spoon as a scoop.

Lewis thought about that last nod. Ordinarily, transient riders just rode in; they rarely knew the man they might work for. Lewis said, "As a matter of fact we need a man. Need a couple of men. I expect you'll stand a good chance."

Joe pushed the empty bowl away. "When will Mister Campbell be back?"

Lewis shrugged meaty shoulders. "I'll tell you something about him, friend. He's as old as gawd but you'd never believe it if you tried to keep up with him. He's usually the last man to ride in after sundown."

Joe said he thought he'd go down to the barn and wait, but the cook, who was a lonely man most of the day, had a better idea. "Naw," he replied. "You any good at checkers?"

Joe was average at one of the wintertime bunkhouse pastimes. "I've played," he answered, and Manuel Lewis got up with surprising alacrity for someone as heavy as he was, and said, "Just set there. I got a board in my room."

Joe sat there.

CHAPTER 18

Rafter C

Manuel Lewis had been correct: the last rider into the yard was James Campbell. He and Gus Acosta put up their saddlestock and split up out front, Gus heading for the washrack around behind the bunkhouse, Campbell heading for the main house to clean up. Joe Bryan ambled over to sit on the veranda to wait for him. Campbell did not know there was a visitor on the ranch until he came out scrubbed and ready for supper. He looked twice, then stopped stone-still. Joe smiled up from the tipped-back chair.

"Good evening."

The older man nodded. "Evening. I didn't know you were out here."

"I wasn't. I was down at the cookhouse letting your cook beat me at checkers for half the afternoon."

Campbell raised his head when Manuel Lewis banged on his triangle summoning all hands to supper, then he pulled a chair around and sat down. "Just visiting, Mister Bryan?"

"Joe will do just fine. No sir, not exactly visiting." Joe started at the beginning and told the cowman everything that had happened back in town at the jailhouse office. Campbell did as he had done other times: he listened without interrupting, but his face gradually took on a sardonic expression.

After Joe finished, Campbell said, "It might be easier to stop Beale than to find Hawk. I told you in town this Hawk, or Aaron Love, or whatever he calls himself these days, can turn into smoke right in front of your eyes. At least that's what the army's scouts used to say. Now, Frank Beale — he wouldn't be hard to find."

Joe said, "Finding Beale isn't the problem. Stopping him is."

James Campbell sat a long time in quiet thought and during that interval Joe studied the older man closely. He thought he detected a hint of that shrewdness Henry Glover had mentioned. Then Campbell faced him and said, "Now then, this is just an idea, Joe. Mind you, I'm only makin' a suggestion."

Joe nodded. In his experience when anyone started out protesting that something had no personal overtones to it, sure as the Good

Lord had made green grass, it *did* have personal overtones.

Campbell made an all-inclusive wave with one arm. "There's been all manner of trouble-makers come out here since I put up these buildings. I'm still here and they ain't." Campbell lowered the arm and shot Joe a swift, appraising glance before flashing a disarming smile.

Joe nodded. Not about what Campbell had just said, but about the truthfulness of what Henry Glover had said about old Campbell. Shrewd. Sly as a damned fox.

"Well now," Campbell continued, "I can tell you where Aaron Love — Hawk, if you like that better — used to have some of his hideyholes. I only run onto them long after the army an' just about everyone else no longer cared about the old goat. But finding him now . . ." Campbell shook his head slowly. "Those are big, deep mountains and he knows everyone yard of them. Finding him so's you can keep the little boy would be damned awful hard, and you might never even see his smoke. Then where would you be?"

Joe nodded again. Not about Campbell's discouraging remarks, but because he suspected all that had been a prelude to something else. He was right.

Campbell settled back in his chair, shoved out his legs and clasped both hands across his flat stomach.

"Like I said, Joe, there's been lots of troublemakers come out here. . . . If Miz Turner would bring the lad to the ranch, believe me, I don't care whether it's the army or a whole herd of reservation policemen, they wouldn't get any closer to the house than that barn down yonder." He dropped his gaze to Joe's face. "I got tough riders, loyal to the brand, an' I got something else — a partnership of fee-lawyers who do work for me now an' then from offices up in Denver." Campbell leaned forward and patted Joe's leg lightly. "You leave them in town — even if you don't try to find old Love — you can expect Beale to come back loaded for bear the next time."

Joe let his breath out very slowly. The idea of having Campbell for an ally appealed to him. The difficulty was that if he mentioned bringing Wes out here where he would be safe, Mary Jane would never hold still for it. She not only had her own home in town, but she had strong principles.

He said, "Mister Campbell, you ever been between a rock and a hard place?"

The cowman laughed. "Never been anywhere else, Joe."

"I just don't believe my sister would do it."

Campbell's eyes widened. "Why not? She'd have everything she wanted out here, and if it's something else, why then, I'd move into the bunkhouse so's she and the boy could have the main house all to themselves." Campbell's gaze became intent. "I want to help her keep the boy. You can ask around, Joe; when someone tries to make trouble for folks I'm fond of, I get downright involved."

Joe wanted to laugh but restrained himself. However, he did say something he thought would be close to the target. "Mister Campbell, tell me straight out: Are you interested in my sister, or in the little boy getting a fair shake?"

Campbell did not even hesitate. "I'm right interested in your sister. I always did think she was prettier than a speckled bird. And nice to boot. A genuine lady. Only she was a married woman. . . . Joe, I'm a lot older'n you so maybe this won't make sense, but when folks I'm fond of have problems, why I just by nature take it personal. Your sister wants to keep the little boy and I think the world of your sister. . . . You understand what I'm gettin' at?"

Joe nodded. "I still don't think Mary

Jane will do it."

Campbell flapped his arms. "Will you ask her?"

"Yes . . . But I really came out here because if I can find Wes's grandfather there's a good chance there won't have to be so much trouble."

Campbell snorted. "If you found him tomorrow, he'd lie in his teeth about the little boy. He was famous for lyin' and sneakin' around as far back as I can remember. If he knew the army and an Indian agent was gangin' up to take the child, I'll bet you a good young horse he'd swear on a ten-foot stack of Bibles he never saw either you or the little boy before in his misbegotten life."

Joe was not ignorant of this possibility. Still, if he could just talk to him. . . .

Campbell sat a long time gazing at the younger man. Finally he arose as he said, "All right. You know Gus Acosta."

"Yeah, I know Gus."

Campbell sighed. "I really can't afford to do this, being short-handed right when it's time to start to gather, but you go talk to Miz Turner and I'll turn Gus loose in the mountains."

Joe stood up slowly. "Gus?"

Campbell nodded briskly. "You don't know

Gus. He's the best tracker and sign-reader I ever had on the ranch. He can pick up sign an Indian would miss. If anyone can find Aaron Love it will be Gus Acosta."

Joe knew Gus was good at tracking, and as he stood there now remembering how unerringly Gus had located those horsethieves even in darkness he also remembered Gus's fierceness. "If he found Hawk he damned well might shoot him. Mister Campbell, I've ridden with Acosta when he's fired up."

"Naw, Joe. That's only when he's after Mexican *bandeleros* or horsethieves. He's got reason to hate both. But not some old ghost wearin' old-fashioned Indian beads and bangles and suchlike. An' I'll give him a hunnerd-dollars' bonus for bringing Love in alive. . . . I'm starved. Let's go get some supper; then you head on back and talk to your sister."

As they were leaving the porch Campbell said, "*If* Love's to be found. If he hasn't taken some notion to keep riding until he's over the horizon. It's going to be real chancy. I'd say a man might be hopeful but he hadn't ought to be *too* hopeful."

After Joe had eaten he got his horse out and saddled him in front of the barn. He was not even thinking about the sorrel horse until Gus Acosta came over to lean and watch the saddling. Like the fat liveryman Gus was a horseman. He considered Red in the late-day gloom and said smiling, "Once I had a horse with that same disposition. Hell of a fine using animal for a fact." Gus ran his eyes up and down the sorrel. "Joe, did he ever buck with you?"

Joe gave the latigo a final tug, looped it and looked across the seat of his saddle at the shorter and much darker man. "Once," he replied. "Why?"

"Well, it's none of my business, but that horse I had was the same disposition. . . . You couldn't put him in a stall. If you took him out of a corral he went along good. If you stalled him he'd get barn sour in half an hour, and when you stepped up he'd buck you off an' run back to the stall."

Joe looked from Gus to the sorrel horse, who was standing perfectly still looking straight ahead, but with his little ears lying back slightly. Joe jabbed him in the ribs with a thumb. Red grunted and braced himself against the looped reins. Gus nodded knowingly. Joe unlooped the reins and walked Red out into the middle of the yard, then turned him first to the left, then to the right. Gus lolled back on the hitchrack watching. He was showing a faint, knowledgeable smile.

Joe reset his hat, ran a thumb under the horsehair cinch and yanked Red around to be cheeked. He glared at the sorrel horse. Red was withdrawn, motionless, clearly waiting. "I'm going to knock the slats out of you," Joe muttered, cheeked the horse, toed in and came down in the saddle. Red did not move. Joe looked back and Gus Acosta's smile widened until white teeth showed in the dusk. "Take a deep seat," he suggested.

Joe hauled his horse sharply to the left to force him to loosen his poised stance, then he pulled him just as sharply to the right, and this time he kept Red moving. He went obediently out of the yard at a fast walk. When Joe looked back, Gus was still leaning on the rack, smiling.

They went all the way back to Springville alternating between a lope and a fast walk. By the time it was possible to make out lights, Red had forgotten whatever had been in his mind back in the Campbell yard.

Hickson was not at the barn when Joe led his horse in from out back, just that wispy old sniffling hostler. He took the reins and held Red while Joe unsaddled him and hauled his rig into the harness room. When the old man came along carrying the bridle and blanket Joe said, "Did you stall him?"

"Yessir."

"Take him out an' put him in a corral. Don't stall him again."

The old man ran a soiled sleeve under his nose, sniffed and without argument turned to do as he had been told. Joe went along to watch. As soon as Red was in a large round corral he dropped down and rolled, first one way then the other. He rolled completely over four times and the old hostler cackled. "Worth forty dollars," he crowed. Joe nodded. Among professional horsemen there was a saying that each time a horse could roll completely over he was worth ten dollars.

He went up to the jailhouse. A lamp was burning, the place smelled of tobacco smoke and hot coffee, but it was empty.

From up in front of the harness works gazing northward, he could see two lamps burning up at his sister's cottage. She and Wes were probably having supper, or maybe supper was finished and she was reading to him in the parlor.

He was tired. That bed he had been sleeping in up there seemed very inviting. Over the past twenty or so years he had not slept up off the ground too often; and when he had, it had been in bunkhouses where old rope springs under a bunk were more often than not worse than the ground.

But he did not want to brace Mary Jane just yet. In fact he really did not want to brace her at all, but there had been merit in Mister Campbell's suggestion — even if it had been an unmistakable bid for his sister's interest.

He struck out toward the lights of the saloon.

If a man came right down to it, what was wrong with Campbell's interest? Being a widow was probably even worse than being a widower — assuming the stories about Campbell having been married before, many years earlier, were true. Her husband had been dead a fairly long period of time; Campbell might be tough, but he had showed heart and humor, and most of all, understanding.

Mary Jane could do a whole lot worse.

Most of the saloon's patrons tonight were townsmen. There were no more than four or five rangemen scattered throughout the smoky room and along the bar. Everyone else was wearing shoes instead of boots.

Marshal Glover was down at the lower end of the bar smoking a cigar and talking to the fat liveryman. Joe walked in the opposite direction, found an opening and eased into it as the harassed barman shot him an inquiring glance. Joe said, "Beer," then looked at the man on his left. It was the paunchy caféman, and evidently he had been here a while. It was not particularly hot in the big old room but he was sweating.

The man to Joe's right was one of the rangemen. He nodded when their eyes met and smiled slightly as he said, "Busy night considerin' it ain't Saturday."

Joe agreed and reached for his beerglass when it arrived. The beer was tepid and the color of used bathwater, but it had a good bite to it, and an even better timed-release of high alcohol content. Joe began feeling better. He leaned to his right and said, "Who do you ride for?"

The relaxed, congenial cowboy's answer was short. "No one. I just rode in this afternoon. Are there any jobs around?"

Joe finished his glass of beer before replying. "Go due west to the Campbell outfit. They might need a man."

The cowboy was about Joe's size, build and age. He nodded thoughtfully. "I'm obliged. If I get a job, I'll hunt you up. It ought to be worth a couple of drinks."

CHAPTER 19

Trouble

Joe's reluctance to face his sister kept him at the saloon until he thought she would be in bed, then he crossed the empty roadway and walked northward.

The cottage was indeed dark. The front door was not locked; it rarely ever was. Joe kicked out of his boots and made it silently to the bedroom. He got ready for bed in the dark and when he was covered and warm, totally relaxed in the body, his mind was still churning so, that sleep did not arrive for some time. But the next he heard, some roosters were raising cain somewhere in town. He opened his eyes and saw the spreading pale stain of dawn.

Breakfast had always been Joe Bryan's favorite meal. This morning was different though, in spite of the fact his sister and Wes chattered at him like a brace of magpies. He waited until Wes had gone out back to work on his fort, and Mary Jane had refilled his cup with black coffee. She refilled her own cup too and sat opposite him. "There is trouble," she said quietly.

He raised his eyes. "Here? Did Beale come back?"

"Joe, I'm talking about you. You didn't say ten words through breakfast."

He looked at the cup again. "I'm not sure it's trouble," he replied without taking his eyes off the cup. "You remember the man who had coffee with us the other day — Mister Campbell?"

"Yes, of course."

"I rode out to his ranch yesterday."

"And? Joe, what in heaven's name is it?"

He lifted the cup and drained it, then sat more squarely on the chair. When their eyes met, though, his resolve weakened. "I went out there to see if he'd might know at all where I could find Wes's grandfather. I had an idea that if I could find him and drag him back here, he could face Beale."

"What did Mister Campbell say?"

"Well, he's got a man who rides for him named Acosta. He's a good tracker. He offered to send him into the mountains to see if he can hunt the old man down."

Mary Jane clasped her hands gently atop the table. "Why are you beating around the bush?" she asked.

"Mary, Mister Campbell wants you to take Wes out to his ranch. . . . Now wait a minute. He's a tough man and he's got a tough riding crew. If Beale went out there, he wouldn't get near the house. Campbell told me that. In fact he said even if Beale sent the army out there for Wes, he'd run them off too."

Mary Jane's gently clasped hands whitened at the knuckles; otherwise she had herself under control. "I'm sure Mister Campbell would protect Wes," she said in a steely voice. "And I think Wes would love it out there, horses and plenty of room and all, but he is doing well right here."

"Mary . . . Mister Campbell wants you to come out there too."

For a long time Joe's sister looked steadily at him, then a tint of pink came into her cheeks. But she didn't speak. Eventually she looked down at her clasped hands and said, "That's kind of him. When he was here in the house a few days back he seemed to be a real gentleman, thoughtful and mannerly and all."

Joe was watching her closely. "You wouldn't want to know what I think, would you?"

She did not raise her eyes. "Yes."

"I noticed it the day he was here. He kept watching you, looking at you."

"Joe, for heaven's sake, Mister Campbell is seventy if he's a day."

"What's that got to do with anything, Mary?" Without realizing it Joe had taken the initiative. His misgivings had disappeared. "He's willing to help you any way he can. You and Wes. Right now I figure we might need all the help we can get — and he even talked about some fee-lawyers who do work for him up in Denver. Mary . . . ?"

She got to her feet to fetch the coffeepot from the stove. When she returned to fill the cups, she still wouldn't look at him, and her face was still pink. Joe thought she looked like a young girl. He had always thought she was pretty, but right now she looked young, too.

He lifted the cup half-way to his face. Mary Jane sat down again, Joe's eyes never leaving her face, not even when he raised the cup all the way and nearly scalded his tongue. He put the cup down quickly. "Damn, that's hot," he exclaimed, and her eyes came up swiftly.

"That's what Wes said the first time I gave him a bath."

Joe remembered. He looked across the table. "I told Mister Campbell I didn't think you'd cotton much to the idea."

"Why did you tell him that?"

"Well," he replied, and lost his train of

thought. "Well, I figured you'd have principles or something. He said he'd move into the bunkhouse with his riders — so you and Wes could have the main house all to yourselves. And if there was anything you needed out there, he'd get it for you."

She gave Joe a startling reply. "That is awfully kind of him. I remember the first time I saw him. It must have been ten years ago. He rode in with his crew on a fine black horse and he smiled at me. I smiled back. I didn't know who he was; well, I had heard of a big cowman named Campbell, but I didn't have any idea that's who smiled at me that day."

Joe left the table to dribble cold water into his coffee cup and returned to his chair.

Mary Jane's cheeks had returned to their normal color. "Joe, maybe it wouldn't look right. What would the ladies of the church society think?"

For Joe, the tirade had not arrived. He had worried yesterday, last night and this morning for nothing. Almost for nothing anyway. "The ladies of the church society don't know what Beale is trying to do, nor that you want to keep Wes."

"Oh yes, they know I want to keep him. We met here yesterday and I told them."

"Told them everything?"

Mary got pink again. "Not quite everything. I didn't mention Frank Beale calling on me and that part of it."

"What did they say?"

Mary smiled. "They all have children. Most of them are grown now but they were upset. They said Frank should be horsewhipped for trying to take Wes away from me. . . . They also wanted to know where you got him."

"What did you tell them?"

"The truth. One of them, Missus Anders — she's one of the founders of the society and she's very old — said she remembered a scoundrel years back called Hawk, but his real name was Aaron Something-or-other."

"Aaron Love. Then they believed the story about Hawk leavin' me with the child?"

"Oh yes. Why shouldn't they?"

"Do you know what a catch-colt is, Mary?"

This time she got more than slightly pink in the face. "Of course. Polite folks don't use the term but I've heard it many times." She paused, eyes widening on her brother. "Joe . . . ?"

"No, confound it, he is not mine. I told you how I got him and that's the gospel truth. But I've heard the term around Springville since I rode in. I thought maybe some of your lady friends might have heard that about me too."

She slowly shook her head. "Nothing like that was mentioned. If they'd heard it they certainly gave me no reason to believe they had."

Joe was relieved even though he was not entirely convinced Springville gossips had not been busy. "About Mister Campbell — " he said, and waited.

Mary Jane's eyes dropped again. "I've been thinking about his offer. What do you think I ought to do?"

"Right now I don't believe what the church ladies might think is as important as keeping Wes. I think Mister Campbell's offer is real decent — and I think he is too."

"Then I ought to go out there?"

"Mary, it's up to you."

"Yes, but you do think that, don't you?"

"Yes."

She raised her eyes, pink again. "All right. Should I lock up the house and hire a rig and drive out there?"

Joe finished the coffee before responding. "Something'll get worked out," he muttered, and arose. "I got to talk to the marshal. I'll be back directly." He reached, roughly patted her hand on the table and left.

He did not have to talk to the marshal and

in fact he did not even want to talk to him. He just wanted to go somewhere, down to the livery barn perhaps, and lean on something, put some loose thoughts together.

However, the luck which had been dogging him since entering New Mexico Territory was waiting for him down at the fat man's place of business. As he strolled in, Marshal Glover was just dismounting from a large gelding. He tossed the reins to the hostler and came toward Joe.

"Have a nice ride yesterday?" he asked, brown eyes penetrating and bright.

"I guess so. Why?"

"I went all over town lookin' for you yesterday afternoon when I figured you'd have got back." Glover folded the gloves under his shellbelt. "One thing you got to say about Frank Beale, he don't let any grass grow under his feet. . . . Come on over to the café with me; I been riding a long while."

Joe did not move. "What about Beale?"

"He went to the army."

"How do you know that?"

"Friend of mine told me. He came up from there yesterday afternoon. He saw Frank and the captain in charge of the off-reservation garrison talking up a blue streak out front of the captain's office at the compound. He only heard Frank say something about the army had to go up here with him because some folks were hiding a reservation Indian." Marshal Glover went silent as two men strode past looking for their horses. When he resumed speaking it was in a lower tone of voice. "He tried to hear the rest of it but couldn't. Then the officer took Frank inside with him."

"Yesterday, afternoon?" asked Joe. "Would the army have ridden out then, or would it have waited until this morning?"

"Most likely waited until this morning. Why?"

"Marshal," Joe said with abrupt intensity, "sixteen miles from there to here, and it's a little short of noon right now."

Glover nodded. "That's why I tried to find you."

Joe turned on his heel without another word and walked very fast up out of the livery barn. He turned northward still hastening, and burst in upon his sister.

"Mary, throw whatever you and Wes'll need into a sack or something and meet me out front in fifteen minutes. . . . Beale is coming back, with soldiers."

She turned and stared, color draining from her face. He did not wait. When he was back on the plankwalk he returned to the livery barn, caught the fat man alone and told him he wanted to hire a buggy with a sound horse between the shafts. Hickson looked at Joe, sensing the other man's tension. He said, "All right. Just remember, Mister Bryan, bring the horse back dry. I don't let out no horses I think someone might use hard. Especially in hot weather."

"He'll come back dry, Mister Hickson."

"You want your sorrel horse too?"

"Yes, tie him behind the rig. I'll wait."

As Hickson walked away Joe went up to the roadway and stood in cottonwood shade studying the landform and the heat-haze to the southeast. There was no dust nor any sign of horsemen. He supposed that if the army figured the matter was important, they'd be here soon, even on a hot day like this.

Hickson led out a big seal-brown, stud-necked Oregon remount mare hitched to a strong, heavy buggy, its red and geen enamel dull and faded.

As Joe climbed to the seat and picked up the lines, Hickson pursed his lips as though in doubt about something. But he said nothing as he watched Joe tool the rig up as far as his sister's house.

Agitated and anxious, Mary Jane handed up two cardboard boxes and a large croaker sack to her brother. She caught the little boy by the arm and propelled him toward the gate, and the last thing she did was lock the door. Then, as she was turning away, she halted, turned back, unlocked the door and hurried inside. When she came out, she was wearing a hat.

They passed Springville's last building, turned west off the roadway and drove across-country. The sun was now directly above them. Occasionally Joe stood up to look back. He still saw no dust, but after a mile or so he could not have seen it anyway. The town buildings blocked his southeasterly view.

Mary gradually relaxed, but she too twisted to look back now and then. Wes had probably been bewildered at the outset, but once the rig was bouncing along behind the trotting remount mare, he grinned with excitement.

The heat began to bear down about the time they were midway. Joe brought the fat man's overweight mare down to a steady walk but she sweated hard anyway.

Mary Jane glanced at her brother over Wes's head. He looked back at her and winked. A little reassured, she raised both hands to fuss with her hat. She was a pretty woman with a complexion of peaches and cream, and naturally curly hair that formed a silvery frame for her face.

Joe was searching the blue-blurred distance for a sign of the big trees growing in a large circle when Wes asked where they were going.

"Out to a cow ranch. You'll like it, Wes," Joe replied.

The child looked up. "Are you an' Aunt Mary going to stay there too?"

Joe was slow with his answer. "Aunt Mary will. I don't know whether I'll stay or not. Maybe for a while I won't be able to." He looked down and winked. "But I'll sure be back as soon as I can."

The big mare had picked up a scent and was walking along with her head up, her ears pointing directly ahead. She had located the yard. Joe saw the trees then too, and a little farther along he saw the buildings.

CHAPTER 20

Campbell's Story

When they arrived at the Campbell ranch Joe drove in and tied up the rig. Manuel Lewis came out of the cookhouse and stood in the overhang shade staring at Mary Jane and the little boy.

The best shade was over there so Joe led his sister and the boy across the yard. When Wes, who was clinging to Mary Jane's hand, came up onto the porch Manuel finally managed a smile, but his greeting reflected his initial reaction. "We never had a little feller on the place before." Manuel looked at Mary. "Nor a real pretty woman."

He held the door for all three to enter his cookhouse. Inside he offered them coffee. Mary Jane's face was flushed from heat. She shot her brother a glance and when he accepted the cook's offer she did also.

Manuel sat them at the long table and went to his huge coffeepot which was always kept hot on the woodstove. While he had his back to them he scraped what remained of his cobbler into a bowl, then brought it to Wes with a spoon and a smile. "Better for a little man than coffee," he said. Wes smiled at him.

The door opened and James Campbell entered. His hat was tipped down to shade his eyes. When he took in the scene at the table, he smiled; it was a very engaging smile.

Manuel brought another cup of java.

Campbell sat down opposite his guests. He was careful not to stare and he addressed Mary Jane's brother when he said, "You're right prompt, Joe."

"Didn't have much choice. Beale's on his way to Springville with some soldiers."

Instead of registering surprise or chagrin, Campbell looked almost pleased. "Is that a fact?" he said. "Well now, that's not very neighborly of him is it?" Campbell turned toward Mary Jane. "Miz Turner, you got nothin' to worry about. This won't be the first time I've had soldiers pokin' around out here, but it'll be the first time in many years."

He watched Wes eating the cobbler for a moment, then said, "I'll move out of the main house, ma'am. There's empty bunks at the bunkhouse. You and the lad can settle in and make yourselves to home." He smiled warmly again. "I'm glad you folks came. Anythin' you lack you let me know, but most of all you and the lad make youselves comfortable. Don't fret."

Joe looked at his sister. Her face was flushed, but this time Joe was unable to tell whether the high color was due to the heat or something else. She smiled back at Campbell. "This is putting you out, Mister Campbell. If we hadn't been desperate — "

"Naw. No such a thing, Miz Turner," the old cowman said, cutting across her statement with a wave of his hand. "To be right honest, I was hopin' you folks'd show up." He laughed. "Doin' the same thing month in an' month out sort of gets a man into a rut. I'm not just glad you came, ma'am. You an' the lad. But I sort of like the idea of Beale comin' too." Campbell faced Joe again. "Lots of folks saw you leave town, did they?"

"I expect so."

Campbell continued, "Then I supposed we can expect Beale out here sometime this afternoon or evening." He stood up looking for the *cocinero*. Manuel Lewis had been listening to every word while peeling spuds. "I expect our guests'll be hungry, Manuel."

Lewis nodded. Campbell smiled at him. "I know it's between meals and all . . . "

The cook's dark features settled into something between resignation and understanding. "It's no bother, Jim."

Campbell faced the visitors. "When you're fed, go over to the main house. I'll take some things down to the bunkhouse."

Mary Jane smiled. "We can't do that, Mister Campbell. . . . We're not going to put you out of your own home. If Wes and I could have a bedroom off somewhere. . . . I'd be happy to have you stay at the house with us."

Wes, who was draining his bowl, was not interested in any of this but the three men were, and looked at Mary Jane. Campbell lifted his hat and reset it, shot her brother a quick look, then said, "That's mighty decent of you, Miz Turner. I won't get in your way." Then he walked out of the cookhouse.

Manuel Lewis turned back to his cooking area as he said, "I'll have something for you in a few minutes. You folks just set there and enjoy the coolness."

Joe went outside. Campbell was over in the barn unsaddling a horse he had rigged out and was now going to corral without having used it. When Joe walked in, Campbell looked up quickly. "Joe, I got to explain something to you. It's been a hell of a spell since I sat at the same table with a woman. Did I say the wrong things over there?"

Joe grinned. "No sir. You handled it very well. Both of you did. I think my sister was as uncomfortable as you were. By the way, the lad's name is Wes."

Campbell nodded. "Wes. I guess I should have remembered." He regarded Joe after slinging his saddle across the pole in front of the harness room. "Sometimes things happen pretty fast," he said.

"Mister Campbell, Mary had already agreed to come out here before I heard Beale was on his way back, so — "

"That's not what I was thinking," Campbell said, leaning on a saddlepole and looking steadily at the younger man. "I was thinkin' of something different. Y'see, I had this in mind a few days back, but it's been my experience that there's a time to mention things an' a time not to. . . . I was thinkin' about offering you the job Al Conley had . . . Rangeboss."

Joe was not entirely unprepared for the offer; he just had not expected it at this time. Marshal Glover had mentioned the job to him, only Joe had surmised that it might be the tophand's job, not the foreman's.

Campbell remained relaxed and watching. Joe had never been a rangeboss but he'd been a tophand several times. He told James Campbell this and the older man nodded. "You can do it. I told you — I've been around a long while." His shrewd gaze hinted at dry humor. "I don't know a blessed thing about little children and maybe not a hell of a lot more about womenfolk, but I know men. Joe, I never yet been mistaken in my foreman."

Joe smiled a little. "I'll make a run at it." He extended his hand and the old cowman walked over and pumped it.

Campbell told him, "I hired another feller this morning. I think you know him. He's out with the other hands; name's Wood Griffin." At Joe's blank look the cowman added, "He said he met a feller in the saloon at Springville who sent him out here. He described you to a tee."

Now, Joe remembered. Wood Griffin must have been that calm, friendly man he'd stood beside at the bar. "It was a shot in the dark, Mister Campbell. He said he was new to the country and needed work so I suggested he come out here."

The older man shrugged. "He's a good hand. I can tell 'em just the way they get off an' on a horse. . . . Well, you'll see him this evenin' at supper. Now then, men who work for me call me Jim. 'Mister Campbell' takes too long to say and it's not necessary anyway."

Joe nodded.

Campbell glanced across the sun-bright yard in the direction of the cookhouse. "Let's talk about the soldiers and Frank Beale," he said. "You got any idea why he's stirrin' up such a fuss over that little — over Wes? I know Beale; he wanted to work for me one time and I've run into him other times." Campbell brought his gaze back to his new rangeboss. "He's a sort of smart-aleck feller with a pretty big idea of himself. Why do you think he's makin' up this trouble?"

Joe told Campbell about the confrontation in Henry Glover's office. Then he too glanced in the direction of the cookhouse and unconsciously lowered his voice. "He . . . they tell me Beale is a married man. . . . He started stopping by my sister's place not long after her husband died. . . . "

Campbell's stare narrowed slightly, and in that very soft way he had of speaking when something bothered him, he said, "Is that a fact?"

"He told Mary he'd bring her things and help her out and all."

Campbell's narrowed eyes grew very still.

" . . . I guess he started trying to get too familiar with her or something. Anyway the last time he came by she told him if he ever pushed his way into her house again she'd shoot him."

The older man's expression changed. Now he looked completely delighted. But when he spoke it was in that same very soft tone of voice. "Good for her. By gawd, Joe, good for her."

Joe went on, "I can understand that he might be mad enough to want to hurt her, but it's hard to believe a grown man would try something like this just to spite a woman — take the little boy away from her."

Old Campbell's eyes drifted to the barn's middling shadows. He was quiet a long while before he started speaking. "I'm goin' to tell you something I don't talk about to another livin' soul. I was married once, Joe. A long time ago. When I arrived in this country there were lots of Indians around. . . . In fact, there was a big Ute rancheria up there where you said you met old Aaron Love. . . . Those was hard times for Indians. Everyone was out to make trouble for them. I wasn't no Indian lover, but still an' all, they never bothered me, never stole horses off me nor killed my cattle. . . . I rode up there a few times. Joe, you never saw such misery. . . . Well, you aren't interested in all that. . . . There was a beautiful Ute woman. . . . I drove up some old gummer cows because those folks were starving. . . . After a time I married the girl." Campbell's gaze drifted farther from Joe Bryan. "Two years later we had a little boy. When he was six months old he died after some missionaries came here an' took him away from his mother while I was on a long drive. . . . When I got back she'd killed herself."

Campbell's gaze came slowly back to the motionless younger man. "Don't you believe for one minute there aren't sons-of-bitches in this world who would take a child from its mother — even of she's not his flesh-an'-blood mother."

Joe did not know what to say, so he said nothing.

Campbell, too, was silent for a long time; then he straightened up off the saddlepole and spoke briskly. "I got an idea, Joe, that if you was to ride out a mile or two and sort of keep watch . . . When you see dust from the direction of Springville you lope back. If the Good lord is with us, by then my riders will be back. . . ."

The look on James Campbell's face was fierce. It crossed Joe's mind that perhaps the old cowman, who certainly would not have forgotten his devastating loss, was now looking forward to meeting Frank Beale to settle his personal score with people who would try to separate a child from those who cared for it.

After Campbell left the barn Joe walked outside to unhitch his sorrel horse from the back of the rig. The heat was particularly noticeable and Joe instinctively raised his eyes; any time heat lay heavily on the land without a breath of air stirring, there usually were clouds.

He saw them far to the northeast. Huge, massive mountains of them. They seemed not to be moving but he knew better. It was going to rain. That thought cheered him a little because as a rangeman he knew that unless summer rains drenched the natural graze and browse, animals would do poorly.

As he saddled up his horse Joe thought on the story James Campbell had told him about the Ute woman and their child. He led Red across the yard to almost the same spot where he had mounted the sorrel the last time he had been in here with Gus Acosta. As he swung up he wondered where Gus was now and whether he'd have any luck locating old Hawk.

He rode due east at a walk. It was too hot to push the sorrel, and as far as Joe knew there was no need to. Even if Beale and his soldier-escort had learned in Springville that Joe, his sister and the little boy had left town traveling across-country in the direction of the Campbell place, they would have to travel very slowly because of the heat. Joe watched closely for dust trails.

CHAPTER 21

Into the Night

If Joe Bryan had learned anything since his arrival in New Mexico Territory, it was that in this very ancient country where there had been people and cultures for many hundreds of years, there seemed also to be forces that either whimsically or deliberately ordered people's lives. There was no dust and there were no horsemen. There should have been — but there weren't. He waited until dusk before turning back.

Maybe the commanding officer had decided not to press on through the heat and had rested his men and animals in town before resuming his manhunt — or childhunt — in the cool freshness of a new day.

He turned back and had ridden no more than a couple miles when he thought he heard a steel horseshoe strike rock off on his left somewhere, to the north.

He became alert instantly. It was improbable that Beale and his escort had skirted far up and around the yard so as to be approaching it from the north under cover of failing daylight. But that was certainly not impossible, so he turned in the direction of the sound he'd heard, walking the sorrel horse quietly and avoiding places he thought might have rocky areas.

It was after seven o'clock in the evening. Visibility remained but it was becoming increasingly limited as Joe and Red picked their way and stopped often.

The next time he heard the sound it was roughly parallel to him but farther west. Placing the two sounds into context he surmised whoever was out there was riding directly toward the ranchyard, so he turned back and aimed for a point of interception north of the yard.

He stopped several times but detected no further sounds. It would not be loose horses; loose-stock had its shoes pulled before it was turned out. But each time he'd heard steel over stone it had been just one horse. If that was Beale and his soldiers, there would have been more than just that one sound each time.

He finally dismounted and led the sorrel. Even in oncoming darkness it was possible to skyline mounted men. Joe wanted to do that to whoever was out there; on the other hand, he did not want the other man to do it to him. In dusk or darkness a lot of riders had been shot out of their saddles for being careless about being skylined.

Then he heard a voice he recognized gruffly say, "Kick that danged Indian horse. Make him come up on the lead shank, you shriveled up old ghost!"

Gus Acosta! Joe halted, dropped the carbine back into its boot and swung into the saddle. He called softly, "Hey, Gus!"

The answer was delayed but eventually it came. "Is that you, Bannion?"

"No. It's Joe Bryan. Hold up."

He found them sitting still, looking in the direction from which he arrived. Joe barely glanced at Gus. He looked intently at the big spotted horse slightly behind Gus being led along by a rope from its bridle to Gus's saddlehorn. The wizened silhouette atop the spotted horse had a bedraggled feather hanging forlornly from the back of his head where the hair had been twisted and knotted. Otherwise, old Hawk did not look different from the last time he and Joe had met. He was still carrying that quiver of arrows and the stubby little bow, as well as a long-barreled old rifle slung fore and aft on his off-side by saddle thongs. His shellbelt had the fleshing knife and old revolver Joe recognized.

When he reached them and stopped, Gus said, "What are you doin' out here?"

Joe explained about Beale and the soldiers. Acosta blew out a big breath. The old wizened man behind him on the tall horse seemed to shrink. Joe looked at him. "You sure got me into a mess, you old devil."

Hawk said nothing. His face was too weathered-dark to be seen well in the failing daylight. Gus lifted his reins. "We can talk at the ranch. I'm as hungry as a wolf." He struck out with Hawk's spotted horse being pulled along. Joe turned in beside the old man. For a while they rode in total silence. Then, when Hawk looked around at him, Joe said, "Why didn't you just tell me you couldn't look after the little boy?"

"Because it wouldn't have done no good."

Joe could not argue with that. It was the truth. He kept riding and finally began a slow recitation of all the things that had happened to him as a result of having Wes with him when he rode into Springville. Old Hawk listened and from time to time nodded his head. When Joe finished, Hawk smiled at him and said, "I never figured all that would happen, mister. I figured you'd look after him. That's why I set around so long talkin' with you. You already said it, I couldn't look after him. I seen you as a godsend. Between the border and Spirit Meadow I run across quite a few folks. Even some emigrants with wagons; womenfolk and other children and all. But they wouldn't have nothin' to do with me so I knew they wouldn't take the little boy. One time I even snuck into a camp at night and put him in among their own pups. . . . They drove off the next mornin' and left him out there in the middle of nowhere hollerin' his head off. I knew you wouldn't abandon him. You'd find him a decent home somewhere and all."

Joe looked at the old man. Up until this moment he'd wanted to get his hands around that old scrawny neck. He was still angry. Actually it was more like fierce indignation than actual anger.

As they rode along, old Hawk made a *wibluta* gesture. "I thought it'd make problems for you, but you could handle them things a lot better'n I could, you being younger and more acceptable in the settlements than I'd be." He made the same little signal again. "Peace," he said, interpreting the handtalk sign. "Y'see, mister? All you went through, you still looked after the child. My guesses about you was right." He placed his hand atop the hornless swell of his old saddle and looked ahead where small orange pinpricks of lamplight showed.

Joe's hostility toward this anachronism of a man faded very gradually. After a while he said, "Hawk? Are you plumb certain you told me the whole truth about why you took the little boy in the first place?"

"I'd swear it on a Bible if I had one. It was the absolute truth. His mother was my daughter an' she died when I was on my way down to see her."

"Why didn't you leave him with his father, the trader?"

Hawk leaned aside to expectorate down the off-side of his horse before answering. It was a purely Indian gesture of total contempt. "He wasn't no good. He never was, from what folks told me down there. He'd hardly buried my girl than he taken a Mex girl to his camp. An' she resented him havin' a little child. She beat on the little boy." Hawk turned his lined, nut-brown face.

"How do you know that, Hawk?"

"Because after I scouted them up for a few days I seen her do it. And with his paw settin' right there at the supper-fire swillin' whiskey from a tin cup."

Joe studied the older man's expression.

Even in poor light there was no denying the expression of honest hatred.

Gus was watching the lamplight up ahead when he almost casually said, "It's the same story he told me, Joe. When we get home what do you want to do with him?"

Joe too watched the lights getting closer. "Chain the old goat in the barn, I guess. . . . Gus?"

"Yeah."

"Mister Campbell hired me on as rangeboss."

Gus still rode facing the lights. "Congratulations. I'm glad he did that. You got the makings, Joe. . . . Now we're only down one man."

"He hired a feller named Wood Griffin too. I met him in the saloon at Springville and sent him out. He got hired."

This time Gus placed one hand on his horse's rump and twisted to look back. "Wood Griffin?"

"Yes. You know him?"

After gazing briefly at Joe he swung forward and said, "No, I never met him, but I know something about him. He was up in Cañon City for a few years."

Joe's eyes widened. "The prison up there?"

"Yeah."

"What for?"

"Mail robbery. There was a lot of talk about him some years back. One thing I remember about that; no one approved of what he did but they had to admit he wasn't no coward. He stopped three bullion stages with army payrolls on them — without firing a single shot at anyone although the gunguards blazed away at him. . . . He was a deadshot, Joe. He shot four spokes out of a front coach wheel an' never missed. Then he told everyone to get out and no one argued with someone who could shoot like that, not even the gunguards. . . . But they caught him. They usually do. And sent him to prison for five or six years, I don't exactly recall for how long. . . . Are you sure he said his name was Wood Griffin?"

"That's what Jim Campbell told me he said his name was."

Gus grunted. "Jim . . . ? Hell, he knows that name as well as I do, Joe. . . . And he hired him?"

"Yes."

Gus rode along without saying another word. Like Joe Bryan, he had some pondering to do. But Gus had been with Campbell a lot longer; his ultimate conclusion, as they came into the yard from the north, was that James Campbell had knowingly hired a deadshot stage robber. And Campbell, who was as good a judge of human nature as Gus had ever seen, would not have done anything like that without his own damned good reason.

They tied up out front of the barn and had off-saddled before anyone knew they were down there. In fact Joe kept Hawk with him as he led his sorrel horse and Hawk's big spotted horse out to be turned into a corral and only knew someone had discovered them when he heard Gus in the barn address someone as "Bannion." Joe tried to remember which rider was named Bannion and failed. As he was turning back to enter the barn, Hawk brushed his sleeve and with an anxious expression spoke in a lowered tone of voice.

"Just a minute . . . There's somethin' I'd like to tell you. The man who owns this place — "

"Yeah, I know," Joe said. "You told me to steer clear of him because he was mean and all."

Hawk nodded vigorously. "Yeah, that too, but what I wanted to tell you was that many years ago he married a Ute woman from the rancheria up at Spirit Meadow."

Joe nodded but did not say he already knew this.

"Well now, she was my wife's sister. . . . Campbell didn't like me. White Indians wasn't look on favorable in them days. Him and I had a set-to up there one time. I didn't like him neither. . . . He knocked me down and I knifed him in the leg. The Utes broke it up. I said I'd stalk him an' kill him."

Joe could still hear Gus talking to someone in the barn and looked impatiently at Hawk. "That was a long time back," he said. "Most likely, Campbell wouldn't even remember it."

Hawk shook his head. "He'd remember it. He was tough, mean, hard-ridin' and hard-livin' man. . . . I'd like you to ask Acosta to give me back my bullets."

Joe frowned. "You mean that gun you're carrying isn't loaded?"

"He emptied it and tossed the gun back to me. He done the same with my bow. Unstrung it. And you see this knife?" The old man drew it from its sheath. It had been snapped off about three inches from the hilt.

Joe's frown deepened. He gazed at old Hawk but was thinking back to Acosta's behavior down at the rock field when they had run down those horsethieves. Acosta had his own peculiar code. Anyone else would have taken Hawk's weapons and just flung them away. Joe shook his head and herded the old man back into the barn, but Gus and a tall, rangy man were out front now leaning on the hitchrack as they talked. They heard Joe coming and looked around. Joe recognized the man called "Bannion." He was a tow-headed, lanky, pale-eyed man. As Joe and Hawk approached, the lanky man eyed old Hawk with unabashed interest.

Gus looked sardonically at Hawk when he said, "I told you, old man — that talk I been listenin' to ever since I came to this country about a ghost hauntin' Spirit Meadow when the moon was full, had to be a lot of crap. . . . Right up until Mister Campbell told me who I was supposed to track down."

For all the stories about him, and his reputation, right now Hawk looked old and frail and small and vulnerable standing among younger and larger men. To Joe he resembled something that the passage of time had left high and dry, like a trout out of water.

Hawk looked straight at Gus when he said, "I tried to tell you back up there — "

"You was sitting out there rocking back an' forth and talkin' to yourself like a little kid," Gus said, eyeing the old man contemptuously. "You didn't even hear my spurs."

Hawk went on talking as though he had not been interrupted. "I tried to tell you my wife is buried up there with the rest of them, and come full moon nights when I'm close by, I ride down and set in the grass and we talk. Otherwise you never would have even found my tracks."

Gus was leaning on the rack looking amused and scornful. He started to answer the old man but Joe cut him off. "Leave him be, Gus."

The lanky cowboy shifted position slightly to stare at Joe, but Gus straightened up saying, "Frank — Jim hired him on as range-boss. . . . Come along, it's been a hell of a tiring couple of days."

Joe watched them both go in the direction of the bunkhouse. He had not wanted to oppose Gus but he felt he'd had to. Hawk brushed his arm again. "I'm obliged," he murmured, and faced the lighted windows of the main house with visible apprehension. "We're goin' over yonder?"

Joe nodded. "Yeah. Wes is over there. He'll recognize you."

"Who is Wes?"

"Your grandson. By the way, what's his real name?"

Old Hawk seemed to be thinking for a moment or two before he answered. "Wes is good enough. Let's go. Campbell will throw a fit when I walk in."

Joe doubted that as he nudged the old man along. "Hawk, someday the boy will want to know his real name."

"It's Wes," Hawk replied, and Joe knew from the old man's tone that it would be pointless to ever ask him again.

CHAPTER 22

Foemen — A Half-Century Later

The child was in bed. Only James Campbell and Mary Jane were in the parlor. Evidently they had been talking, enjoying a relaxed visit, because when Joe walked in with old Hawk his sister had been smiling.

They both looked at old Hawk. Joe related how Gus had found him at Spirit Meadow. Campbell seemed hardly to be listening. His gaze was fixed upon the old man in the bizarre attire with the drooping feather hanging down the back of his neck. He did not arise as he pointed to chairs and said, "Set."

Neither Joe nor Hawk moved.

Campbell eyed them a moment longer, then arose and without a word left the room. Mary Jane watched him go and, sensing an awkward and embarrassing situation, also arose. But she smiled when she offered them chairs, and finally Hawk went to sit down. Joe remained standing until Campbell returned with two glasses of watered whiskey. He handed each man a glass and put a hard look on Hawk before returning to his chair. Without looking around he said, "It's been a while, Aaron."

Hawk did not touch the watered whiskey. "A few weeks," he replied dryly, and this time Campbell turned. Joe thought he saw a faint smile in the old squawman's eyes. "Yeah, a few weeks, Aaron . . . Why'd you steal your girl's boy?"

Hawk looked into the glass he was holding before replying. "Because his mother died and his paw took in a Mex girl who beat him."

Campbell continued to stare at Hawk. "And you thought you could do better by the lad?"

Hawk met Campbell's gaze this time. "No. But I thought maybe I could find someone else who would. . . . You ever go up to Spirit Meadow, Jim?"

"No. No reason to."

Hawk tasted the whiskey and put the glass aside gazing at Joe's sister. "How's Wes?" he asked.

She hung fire over her answer. "Fine. At first he didn't talk, but now he's fine."

Hawk nodded at her and looked up at Joe

Bryan, who had not taken a chair and was standing hipshot near the door with his hat hanging from one hand. "She's your sister."

It hadn't been a question, rather it had been a statement, but Joe nodded anyway — and a faint, disturbing thought came to him. "I thought you were going out of the country, Hawk."

The old man studied Joe's face. "Did I tell you that up yonder? Maybe I did. But no, I didn't want to leave."

"So you scouted around Springville."

Hawk did not deny it. "To make certain I hadn't misjudged you is all. The little boy needed more than I could ever give. I snuck around a little, mostly at night but sometimes in daylight. And I figured it out. You said you was going down to Springville because your sister lived there. . . . I went down the alley one afternoon and watched from inside an old shed. The boy was happy. He even had a new pair of boots with toe-caps. Folks don't spend that kind of money on a little boy they don't want, do they?"

Campbell left the room again, and when he returned this time he had two more glasses. One was nearly all water. He gave that one to Mary Jane, and smiled into her inquiring eyes before returning to his chair. When he was settled he spoke in a slow, measured tone of voice.

"Aaron, you didn't make good on your threat."

Hawk settled back slightly in the chair. "No, I never did. What you did was foolish. What I did wasn't much better. Only I didn't start that fight, Jim. You did. Anyway, how could I keep my word? Our women were sisters."

Campbell nodded as though he had long ago arrived at this same conclusion. "What about after the massacre, Aaron? They were both dead by then."

Hawk sipped a little more whiskey and Joe, who was watching both older men, thought Hawk's naturally ruddy coloring was beginning to redden slightly. Hawk probably did not have many opportunities to drink whiskey back in the mountains.

Hawk answered Campbell softly. "Time passes. Things commence to look different. You wasn't as important to me after the massacre. . . . I go out there on full moon nights and we talk. Have you ever talked to your woman, Jim?"

Campbell shot a quick glance at Mary Jane, who was doing as her brother was doing, watching them both and listening. Campbell reddened slightly too as he curtly replied, "No. How can a man talk to someone who's been dead so long?"

Hawk's answer sounded to Joe Bryan like the statement of a man with an unshakable conviction. "You can't, Jim. You brought her down here. She never saw the people again. I can: I talk to my woman. She never left the meadow. She never will leave it."

Campbell shot the old man a bleak glare. "You're not making any sense, Aaron."

Hawk let that go by and sipped more whiskey. Then he put the glass from him and said, "I don't want to argue with you again. Why did you send the Mexican after me?"

Campbell was back on safe ground again. "Because an Indian agent wants to take the lad to the reservation. He's comin' tomorrow with soldiers."

Hawk's permanently squinted eyes widened. "Here? In this yard?"

"Yes," replied James Campbell. "Aaron, your daughter was a half-breed. The little boy is what — a quarter?"

Hawk nodded.

Campbell accepted that. "Quarter-breeds ain't reservation Indians."

Hawk nodded again, still silent. He watched Campbell's face with strong interest.

Campbell shifted in the chair so he would not have to turn his head each time he looked at Hawk. "I wanted you here when the agent rides in with his soldiers. You're the lad's blood-kin, his grandfather. I want you to tell the soldiers who the lad's parents were. That's all."

Hawk had not taken his eyes off James Campbell, neither had he spoken. He did not seem ready to speak now until Mary Jane said, "He's such a good little boy, Mister Love. You said you wanted him to have a decent chance. I want to give him that chance. Will you help me?"

Hawk eyed the two-thirds empty glass but did not reach for it. He looked askance at Mary Jane, then at her brother over by the door. He answered her while looking at Joe. "The army has a bounty on my head. Why didn't you tell me this is what Jim wanted?"

Joe had not deliberately deceived the old man, but he realized it must seem that way. He looked away from Hawk to Jim Campbell, then back to Hawk again. "All I knew, Hawk, was that you could keep them from taking Wes."

Jim Campbell straightened in his chair. "No one's going to take the boy anywhere. . . . Aaron?"

Hawk swung his attention back to the cowman. "They'll haul me off to prison, Jim."

Campbell said nothing. No one did. Not until Hawk fingered a torn place in his dirty old hide shirt. Then it was Joe who spoke.

"Hawk — how long ago was it? Forty, fifty years? None of the soldiers who'll be here tomorrow were even born then. If there was a bounty on you that long ago . . . Hawk, they don't have any idea you'll be here when they ride in, an' I'll bet you a good horse even their officer never heard of any bounty on someone named Aaron Love."

The old man listened to Joe but was looking at Mary Jane. When Joe finished, Hawk smiled at her. "All right. I'm too old anyway. In the mountains maybe I'd live another few years. In their prison I won't live half that long. But it's all right. You raise my grandson. See to it he grows into an honest man."

Mary Jane's eyes filled. James Campbell saw that and turned toward Hawk. "No one'll take you out of this yard if you don't want to go. Not the damned army and not anyone else."

Hawk cast a slow look in the cowman's direction, then smiled at Joe. "Let's go down to the barn. You got some chains down there?"

It was Joe's turn to get red in the face. He

dumped the hat on his head as he said, "Is your word any good, Hawk?"

"Yes."

"You tell me you'll be down there in the morning and we won't use any chains."

Hawk arose. "I'll be there."

Mary Jane rose from her chair and offered her hand to old Hawk. "Don't make any noise. I'll show you your grandson." Hawk took her fingers and allowed himself to be led out of the room. Moments after their departure Jim Campbell got up and looked at Joe. Without a shred of doubt he quietly said, "That was painful."

Joe nodded. "Will he keep his word, Jim?"

"Yes . . . Joe, damn — I sure made a fool of myself, didn't I?"

"I didn't think so."

"Well, I did. I didn't have to act like our fight happened yesterday. . . . He looks sort of frail, don't he?"

"Yes, but then he's old."

Campbell turned to put the glass atop a small table, then straightened around. "He's old and they're all gone but him. You know, this is the first time I ever saw him when he didn't have Indians around him. Funny thing, years back he seemed to me to be nothin' more than a damned squawman. That wasn't right either. He was an Indian back then too, only now it's more noticeable. How can somethin' like that be when he was born a white man?"

Joe had no answer.

Campbell may not have expected one. He walked to the big stone hearth and faced around from it. "Well, Joe, sundown is coming. One of these days he's goin' to sit down with his back to a tree up there, and die."

Joe nodded. He did not doubt that.

"The Spirit Meadow he talked about. I own it. My property line runs east-west about three quarters of a mile north of the meadow." Campbell gripped both hands behind his back as he stood looking across the lighted room at Joe. "I can't run cattle up there. You know why?"

Joe nodded. "Bears, wolves, mountain lions."

Campbell bobbed his head curtly. "I'm a cattleman. What I can't graze cattle an' horses over is worthless to me. . . . I'm going to give him that damned meadow. . . . Trouble is, he's too old to build a decent cabin up there."

Joe raised a hand to gently rub the tip of his nose. "I've built my share of log houses. Only I wouldn't have the time if I'm on full-time, would I?"

Campbell's gaze neither wavered nor blinked. "Yes, you would. That'd be part of your job. But first we got to finish the gather. After that we'll have maybe six weeks before we commence the drive to rails-end. You an' maybe Kincaid and Hudson could go up there."

"Are you goin' to tell him all this, Jim?"

"Yes . . . I feel like gettin' drunk tonight. Old Aaron and me. Talk old times. Maybe get a little mad about a lot of things all over again."

"Go ahead," Joe said, faintly smiling at the vision of Campbell and old Hawk getting drunk around the kitchen table. It probably would not take much to do that to either of them.

"I can't," Campbell said abruptly, yanking Joe's thoughts back to the parlor.

"Why not? Not enough whiskey left?"

Campbell snorted. "I got a full case of malt whiskey in the kitchen cooler. I can't do somethin' like that with your sister and the lad in the house."

Joe went to a chair and sat down. "Well, after the soldiers leave tomorrow, then. Or maybe you could go up to Spirit Meadow when the work's done and then — "

"Not while your sister's here, Joe. What

kind of a feller would ride off to get drunk when — he's got a houseguest like her?"

Joe did not look up when he said, "You got a real problem, Jim." Then he arose as Hawk and Mary Jane returned. Her eyes were bright. She smiled at Jim and Joe.

Old Hawk looked at them too. His expression was different from what it had been. He said, "Good. Better than I hoped and schemed for it to be . . . Jim? I'll be down at the barn in the — "

"Wait a minute, you darned old billy goat," said Campbell. "Sit down and be patient for a little while. . . . Mary Jane . . . ?"

She saw Joe's faint grin and read it correctly. "Jim, it's been a very trying day. . . . Good night, gentlemen." As she turned to go back down the dark hallway Campbell squinted after her then slowly faced her brother.

"Does she read minds?"

Joe's smile blossomed. "You sure told the truth when you said you didn't know much about womenfolk, Jim."

Campbell's eyes narrowed. "And you — you know all about them, I expect."

"No. I don't even know as much as you do. But I know this one. Even when we were kids she had a knack for knowin' when it was time to walk out of a room."

Campbell drifted his gaze to old Hawk, who had been looking from one to the other. He cleared his throat and shifted his stance on the stone hearth. He also regripped his hands behind his back.

"Aaron . . . I'm not going to say I was wrong for startin' that fight."

Hawk accepted that. "I know that. You never will either. You wouldn't admit to bein' wrong if your life depended on it."

Campbell's expression turned harsh and for a long moment he was silent as he regarded old Aaron Love. Joe watched him struggle with himself. Campbell finally cleared his throat again. "Aaron, you damned old scoundrel . . . Did you know I own the land for nearly a mile north, east and west of Spirit Meadow?"

Hawk hadn't known it. Property lines appeared to be of no interest to him. "No. But I ain't surprised. You always was a land hog."

Joe saw the stain of anger returning to Campbell's face, but to the cowman's credit he retained control. "You better stop insulting me," he said bleakly.

"Why? You insult me, Jim."

"Because, you blasted old rack of bones, I'm going to give you Spirit Meadow. That's why."

Hawk's eyes widened for the second time since he'd entered the house. He looked to Joe Bryan as though he was unable to speak, or even to breathe.

Campbell took advantage of Hawk's stunned silence. "All of it. I'll have my fee-lawyers in Denver draw up the deed. I'll even send someone up there to survey it. It's yours free and simple. . . . Aaron, when we're through making the summer gather, Joe here and a couple other riders will go up and help you put up a decent log house."

Hawk turned very slowly to look at Joe, then just as slowly he turned back toward Jim Campbell. "You're drunk," he said. "Jim Campbell, you're drunk."

Campbell glowered. "Drunk? You never saw me drunk in your misbegotten life."

Hawk's narrow shoulders slumped inside his old doeskin shirt. "Jim . . . Why would you do that? I never been your friend."

Campbell shifted uncomfortably. "Don't ask damn-fool questions," he said; then, at the stricken look on the old man's face, he cleared his throat again and smiled. "Aaron . . . that's where your heart's been for fifty years. Mine's been down here. I don't want anyone else to have it but you . . . Joe?"

"Yes?"

"Why don't you go on down to bed. You had a hard day of it."

Joe nodded and reached for the door latch. He nodded again to them both and walked out into a cold night. The bunkhouse was dark. So was every other building except the main house. He reset his hat and went down off the porch. Midway toward the bunkhouse it crossed his mind that they would sure-as-gawd get drunk. That idea did not dismay him at all, in fact he rather liked it. What made him wince was a hunch that if they sat with a bottle in the kitchen and got to arguing, they'd make a ruckus and waken his sister and Wes. Mary Jane was not accustomed to drunken men.

Well, maybe she would understand. If she didn't, he would explain everything to her in the morning.

CHAPTER 23

The Visitors

They did not raise a ruckus even though they both got well enough sauced-up to have trouble focusing on each other, but Joe would not have had an opportunity to explain things to his sister anyway.

Before dawn Joe was out back at the wash-rack waiting for big, easygoing Wood Griffin to finish shaving. Gus Acosta was waiting too, but being an impatient man, he walked out a ways to admire the paling sky and the promise of sunlight. While he was standing there, old towel slung over one shoulder, the towheaded, lanky man named Bannion came out of the rear of the barn, saw Gus and headed briskly for him.

When they met, Bannion said something neither Joe nor Griffin could hear, then they split up, Bannion heading back toward the barn, Gus making a beeline for the porch where Joe was standing.

"Company coming," he said, looking Joe in the eye.

They left Griffin at the washrack and hiked around the north side of the bunkhouse until they could see miles of softly dawnlighted country eastward behind the cookshack. Bannion sauntered from the barn to join them. He said, "Y'know, I grew up in Missouri. My pappy an' uncles taught me early to watch out around soldiers wearin' blue. Strange how early impressions stay with a man, ain't it?"

Joe and Gus watched the distant party of riders in total silence. Joe was trying to pick out the Indian agent. The distance was too great so he made a guess at the number of soldiers and was surprised there weren't more. It did not seem that there were more than eight or ten. For some reason he had been expecting a whole herd of soldiers, like a small army. A regiment maybe, certainly no less than a company.

Gus nudged Joe. "You better go tell the boss. I'll go around the yard."

Joe went over to the main house where a spindrift of whitish smoke was rising from the kitchen stovepipe. Mary Jane was at work. He rattled the door. When his sister opened it smiling at him, he said, "Tell Mister Campbell they are coming, Mary."

Her smile vanished. She stepped out and

looked across the miles of open country, saw them, and went back inside forgetting to close the door. Joe closed it for her, then stood on the porch watching the horsemen. They were a good two miles out, maybe a little more than that. In the glass-clear atmosphere of first daylight they seemed closer, and finally, he could count them. Ten behind and one out front. There were two riders out front but only one wore a blue uniform.

Campbell came from the house buckling an old shellbelt around his lean middle. The holstered Colt had hard rubber grips with a rearing horse on them. The horse had an arrow in its mouth. Those were standard grips, the kind that had come with the gun. They were worn almost smooth.

He squinted, watched briefly, then hauled out a blue bandana and lustily blew his nose. As he was pocketing the bandana he spoke to his rangeboss while regarding the riders. "A squad of them, it looks like. That'll be Beale in the brown suit."

Joe squinted. He could not make out a brown suit.

Campbell stood watching for a long time before he faced Joe. "Make sure the boys know. . . . Tell that new man I'd like to see him over here. And Joe — Aaron ain't in the barn. I rolled him into a spare room last night. He was too drunk to find his behind with both hands."

Joe nodded, eyeing the older man. "It'd sure be better if he was sober when he talks to them, Jim."

"He'll be sober. You go do what I told you an' I'll commence pouring black java down old Hawk, and get Mary Jane to fill him with grub."

Joe found Wood Griffin standing in the barn doorway with the others, thumbs hooked in his shellbelt. He, Gus Acosta and Bannion looked as though they almost relished this. Jack Hudson and Jim Kinkaid didn't.

Griffin nodded when Joe relayed Jim's message and started for the main house. Gus watched him go in. He wagged his head and shot Joe a rueful look.

"I don't know that Jim ought to set Griffin onto those men."

"What makes you think he will?" asked Joe.

"I don't know that he will — but Jim's a bearcat when he's roiled up."

The lanky, towheaded man was leaning against a door balk watching the riders when he said, "Naw. He's not goin' to do anything like that, Gus."

Gus's dark face turned swiftly. Bannion, who was taller, smiled downward at the shorter and thicker man. Gus said, "Then why'd he call Griffin over there? You know who Griffin is?"

Bannion continued to smile. "Sure I know. Gus, I'll bet you my saddle against your saddle Jim won't start no war. You want to bet?"

Gus either knew Bannion too well to wager with him, or worried that Bannion had figured out something he had overlooked. "No bet," he replied. "Why won't Jim fight 'em?"

"Because," drawled the lanky man, "he's got that lady and the little boy in the house. That's why."

Kinkaid said quietly, "I sure hope you're right."

But their hope appeared to be without much actual foundation when Wood Griffin emerged from the main house carrying a long-barreled Winchester rifle. He did not come toward the men in front of the barn but went down behind the bunkhouse, past the rear corrals, up into the barn and climbed the pole-ladder to the loft. He did all this without even looking at the other riders.

Gus looked bitterly at Bannion. "You still want to bet?" he asked, but the approaching horsemen were much closer now and Bannion's full attention was upon them. He said, "Who is that feller in the brown city suit and the flat-brimmed hat?"

Joe answered. "Frank Beale. He's Indian agent to the reservation."

Soon Beale and the soldiers were nearing the upper end of the yard. Manuel Lewis come out onto his raised front porch and leaned a long-barreled scattergun against the railing. He pulled an old chair around, sat down and cocked his feet over the railing.

Overhead, Griffin gently pushed open the little loft door. No one looked up even though they plainly heard the hinges squeak. Jim Hudson said, "Countin' that feller in the city suit, they got us outnumbered."

Bannion reiterated his earlier line, in the same dead-calm, drawling tone of voice. "Outnumbered don't matter. Push ain't goin' to come to shove."

The soldiers were not youngsters. Neither was their officer, who was dusted like the rest of them from the long ride. Frank Beale saw the slouching armed stockmen in front of the barn and leaned to speak nervously to the barrel-chested officer. Instead of answering, the officer, gray-headed and burned brown from field duty, kept looking upward. "It must be just an accident, Beale," the officer was saying, "but the loft door is open."

The Indian agent looked up. Meanwhile the officer spoke again, very dryly this time. "During the war we learned real early never to go into a yard where the loft door was hanging open."

Evidently the barrel-chested officer had chosen to ignore his experience about loft doors this time, because he rode directly to the rack out front of the barn, nodded to the wooden-faced rangemen standing in the front barn opening, and loosened his reins as he turned and spoke quietly to a grizzled, red-faced sergeant. "Dismount the men," he said.

The only sound was of horses, saddlery and metal. The officer wore gloves which he peeled off while looking at the men across the rack from him. Frank Beale looked at them too, his gaze lingering longest on Joe Bryan. "That's the man," he told the officer. "The one in the middle. Joe Bryan. He's the one who threatened to shoot me in the marshal's office. It's his sister has the Indian boy."

The officer tucked away his gloves and regarded Joe from a face which was resolute, but not hostile. "Mister Bryan," he said quietly, with a hint of briskness. "I have a warrant for the Indian boy." He was loosening his coat to reach inside it when a harsh call from the porch of the main house distracted them all.

"Beale! You got business to transact on my land, you transact it with me!"

The soldiers turned, as did Beale and the officer. Beale spoke aside to the officer. "Mister Campbell. He's the one I told you about yesterday."

The officer lowered his hand, regarded James Campbell with unruffled calm, then said, "Sergeant, water the horses, loosen cinches. Stay apart and wait. Beale, come with me."

Joe admired the man's ability to control the situation around him. He watched Beale and the officer cross the yard in the direction of the main house. The grizzled sergeant asked about water. Joe bobbed his head at Bannion, and the lanky man gestured for the troopers to follow him down the south side of the barn toward the corrals and troughs out back.

Not a word was said, although the rangemen eyed the individual troopers with frank curiosity, and got back an answering stare from the soldiers.

"Joe!"

Joe turned to find Campbell beckoning him. Before walking away he said, "Gus, don't let anyone do anything foolish. . . . Keep an eye on the cook and that shotgun."

Instead of acknowledging that he had heard, Gus asked a question. "Where is that old devil with the feather down his back?"

Joe was walking away and did not reply.

Gus flapped his arms and took Hudson and Kinkaid with him as he slouched around back where the army animals were being tanked up. Bannion and the scarred, granite-jawed, graying sergeant were sharing Bannion's tobacco sack. They had lighted up by the time Gus and his companions got back. The sergeant cast an appraising glance in their direction, then ignored them to turn back to Bannion as he said, "What'n hell is this all about?"

Bannion trickled smoke, pale eyes fixed almost indulgently upon the barrel-built noncommissioned officer. "There's a little boy over at the house. That feller in the brown suit says he's an Indian and belongs on the reservation. Didn't your captain tell you?"

The sergeant regarded Bannion and Gus caustically. "When did an officer ever tell an enlisted man anything? You gents never been in the army, I can see that. All he told me yestiddy was to round up a squad ready to ride. That's all."

CHAPTER 24

A Matter of Leeway

There was as much tension inside the main house as there had been out in the yard.

The officer was businesslike with James Campbell and he was courtly toward Mary Jane, whose face reflected strain and dread as she listened to the captain's words.

He was reaching inside his tunic as he addressed James Campbell. "I have a warrant for one Indian child signed by my commanding officer." He brought forth a folded paper but did not offer it to Campbell. His gaze was uncompromisingly direct. Campbell's was the same. "Mister Beale here told us about his earlier difficulties trying to claim the Indian child. I hope I don't encounter the same thing." Now, finally, he offered the warrant to Campbell.

The old cowman did not accept it. The captain colored slightly and let his hand drop to his side as he and James Campbell eyed one another. It put Joe in mind of a pair of stray dogs taking each other's measure and being careful about it.

The captain finally said, "Where is the child, Mister Campbell?"

Mary Jane looked pleadingly in the old cowman's direction. Joe saw this but Campbell didn't; he was looking steadily at the soldier when he said, "He's here, if that's what's worrying you. But you don't take him."

The officer did not even blink. "I said I hoped this could be done without trouble, Mister Campbell," and the cowman's answer was as flinty as his previous remarks had been. "There won't be, Captain. You just mount up your troops and ride away."

Joe was near the door behind the captain and Beale. The officer threw him a glance. He returned the officer's look impassively. The officer tried again.

"Mister Campbell, I have a warrant. I didn't draw it up or sign it, my commanding officer did. . . . I'll tell you this — the idea of the army running down a child struck me as being quite a comedown. But I obey orders."

Joe thought it was a fair statement by a man who wished to avoid trouble. He looked at the old cowman. His face was as granite-set in opposition as ever, but when Campbell spoke, his voice was not quite as harsh. "You got leeway, Captain. I never been a soldier but a long time back I was around the army quite a bit. Officers are sent out with troops under orders, just like you said — but they got leeway, they got discretion."

The burly officer did not appear to appreciate that statement. Putting his head slightly to one side, he regarded Campbell wryly. "Do they, for a fact?"

Campbell made a death's-head smile. "Yes sir, they do. . . . You recollect a man named General George Armstrong Custer?"

Joe saw the back of the captain's neck begin to redden. Brevet-General George Custer's glaring bad judgment in using discretion was something the army would never forget.

"What does that have to do with my orders?" he asked, and the cowman was waiting for exactly that question.

"You take the lad out of my yard by force, and the army'll have cause to ponder about allowing officers leeway."

"You intend to fight us, Mister Campbell?"

"Massacre would be more like it. We knew you were comin'. We been gettin' ready for you."

The officer gazed thoughtfully at the older man. He was thinking of the loft door. He blew out a big breath and turned toward

Frank Beale, but the Indian agent was staring nervously at Mary Jane. Joe got the impression Beale wished now that he had never pushed for this kind of a showdown.

Campbell spoke again. In Joe Bryan's view, the old devil had been following some private battle plan, and thus far he had done quite well. "Now then, Captain — with your discretion to act independently, I'd like you to meet an old friend of mine." Campbell did not look away but he raised his voice slightly. "Mister Hawk!"

From the gloomy hallway old Hawk appeared, and Joe's eyes widened. The feather was gone, his iron-gray mane of coarse hair had been trimmed and he was wearing a suit that fit him perfectly for height, even though it was slightly loose on his skinny frame. He walked up beside James Campbell and solemnly nodded without taking his eyes off the army officer. Campbell introduced them. Neither man offered a hand but they both acknowledged the introduction by nodding. Campbell said, "Captain, this is the little boy's grandfather. His daughter was the child's mother and she died."

Joe stopped breathing, but Campbell said no more about the boy's parents. He did not mention a living father, but went right on speaking as though the only important thing was what he had said about the mother.

"Mister Hawk lived alone in the mountains. He had no way to look after a small child." Campbell looked in Mary Jane's direction for the first time in a while, and smiled at her. "This here lady is raising Wes — Wes is the little boy." Campbell's eyes went to Beale's face and remained there, and Joe held his breath again; but, as before, Campbell said nothing of Beale's attempts to force himself on the widow. Instead, he said, "She's doing a fine job. The child loves her. She's a widow-woman, Captain. She needs the child as much as he needs her. . . . Now then, would you say Mister Hawk is an Indian?"

The officer eyed old Hawk, who was weathered brown with blue eyes and non-Indian features. But instead of replying to the question the captain said, "Go on, Mister Campbell."

The cowman had handled the situation very well up to this point. He smiled at Joe's sister and asked her if she would fetch Wes to the parlor. As she was leaving the room Frank Beale licked his lips and leaned to say something to the officer, and from the doorway Joe Bryan coughed slightly, bringing Beale's attention around. Joe smiled innocently into the

Indian agent's eyes and lowered his right hand to the sawhandle of his holstered Colt and closed his fingers around it.

Frank Beale faced abruptly forward and swallowed.

Mary Jane returned with Wes holding her hand. The child looked from the forbidding, erect figure in dusty blue to Frank Beale, whom he recognized, then back to the officer. He edged in closer to Mary Jane, his golden coloring fading to a frightened white.

Campbell looked down and winked. Then he faced the officer again. "There is your full-blood, Captain."

It was quiet enough in the parlor to hear a pin drop as the soldier stood looking at the little boy whose dark, curly hair was sweat-damp over his forehead.

The soldier studied Wes for a long time and Joe saw the color coming into his neck again. But he said nothing until Mary Jane led Wes to the chair where she had been sitting; the boy sank down, and leaned against the chair's side holding her hand in a tight grip.

The captain finally looked from the child to Frank Beale, who was now sweating noticeably. Beale pushed up a feeble look of righteous indignation. "Don't let the light skin fool you," he said. "Like I told Butler and that fool of a lawman in Springville, I can produce two dozen squaws nearly that fair-skinned."

The officer finally spoke, softly and ironically. "With curly hair, Mister Beale? I've been on the border a long time. I've brought in renegade Indians and break-outs by the score. . . . Never with curly hair. Not even when they're half-breeds. . . . Mister Beale, I'd like a word with you on the porch." The officer looked at Wes again, then at Mary Jane, Campbell even old Hawk, before turning to lead the way out of the house to the shaded porch. Beale followed him like a puppy.

Joe leaned to quietly close the door after them. He looked at his sister. She appeared to him to be on the point of collapse, but her jaw was set and her eyes were unwaveringly resolute. Joe blew out a big breath, and wondered what would have happened if things had turned out differently.

He had not time to reach a conclusion. Old Hawk sat down, ran a bony finger between his gullet and the buttoned white collar around his neck, and said, "Jim . . . sure could do with a drop from the kitchen."

Campbell nodded but made no move to leave the parlor. He went over to rumple

Wes's hair, and lean down and smile into Mary Jane's face. "I told you," he said.

She smiled back with misting eyes. "I know you did, and I shouldn't have doubted you. . . . Will they leave now?"

Campbell turned just his head. "Joe, see what they're up to."

The voices Joe heard as he opened the door to pass beyond it were low, but intense. They paused the moment someone came from the house. The captain was red in the face. Beale looked shaken and distinctly uncomfortable. He looked around as Joe came out, but the officer did not take his eyes off the Indian agent. His lips were flattened, his nostrils flared, his eyes were smoky. He ignored Joe as though he did not exist. There clearly was just one thing on the officer's mind.

In a leashed tone of voice, he said, "That's no excuse, Beale. There is no excuse for this. As I said, have you any idea how this will look when I report back? The colonel will demand a written report. . . . Twenty or more miles to get out here, twenty or so miles to get back to the post — a detail, an officer, an utterly useless excursion — and you had seen that child. You knew he was not a full-blood, not even a halfbreed. What made you do this?"

Beale shifted his stance, fished a white cloth

from a coat pocket and mopped his face and neck, all without meeting the angry officer's eyes.

"Beale, what possessed you? You saw the warrant. It specified a reservation Indian. So why did you let this farce go on? I can't for the life of me understand this. . . . Well, say something, will you?"

Joe left the porch; if Beale responded to the officer he did not hear it. Down in front of the barn the riders had been killing time, but at the sight of Joe heading their way, they straightened up.

Gus asked, "Well . . .?"

Bannion interrupted. "You lost your saddle, Gus."

Gus turned on him. "We never bet. . . . Joe?"

Joe was unsure of the final outcome but he told them in detail how their employer had adhered to what Joe was convinced was a preplanned strategy. He finished by jerking his head in the direction of the porch where the officer and Frank Beale were still standing. "The captain's mad as a hornet, an' I got to agree with him. Beale's got to be a complete darned fool to think he could do this. I don't happen to think he's an idiot, so I got to wonder like the captain's doin' why he kept trying."

"You got any idea?" Gus asked, and Joe raised a hand to gently rub the tip of his nose. He did not answer the question.

A quiet voice asked a question from the shadowy gloom deeper inside the barn. "Now what?"

They all looked over to where Wood Griffin was standing at the foot of the loft ladder, leaning on the Winchester rifle. Joe answered him. "We got to wait, but after listenin' to that officer I don't think they'll try to take the little boy. All the same, you better climb back up there."

Griffin did not move. "It's a hundred and twenty degrees under the roof and I'm dry as a cotton boll."

Bannion turned without a word, went down to his saddle, unslung a canteen from the horn and handed it to Griffin. Then he grinned and jerked his thumb upward.

Griffin started climbing, holding the rifle and canteen in the same hand. Just before his head disappeared through the opening he said, "Hey, Joe — thanks for sendin' me out here to work cattle. So far all I've seen is a lot of country, some horses, cows off a hell of a distance — and soldiers." He was climbing and out of sight by the time the burly sergeant left his troopers and headed for the porch where Beale was slumped against an overhang upright and the officer was lighting a thin cigar. Whatever they had discussed over there had evidently been concluded.

The captain watched his noncommissioned officer cross to the foot of the porch before removing the cigar and looking down at him as he said, "Water the stock, cinch up and get mounted. I'd like to reach Springville before dark . . . Sergeant?"

"Yes sir . . . That's all, sir?"

The captain trimmed ash with a finger. "That's all."

The sergeant stood his ground looking up. "Sir? Anyone goin' back with us?"

This time the officer plugged the cigar back between strong teeth. "Yes . . . Mister Beale. No one else. Be ready when I come down to the barn."

The sergeant nodded and turned to walk back the way he had come.

For a long time the officer stood smoking the shade gazing out over the heat-blurred countryside, then he turned without even glancing at the slouched man on the porch railing, and went back into the house.

CHAPTER 25

Dust and a Dappled Horse

Three days later Marshal Glover rode out early, before the heat had arrived. Joe was out with the riding crew but James Campbell was in the yard. As Glover dismounted, the old cowman cocked an eye at him and asked, "Did that soldier-officer see you before headin' down-country?"

Glover was looping his reins as he replied. "Yeah. We sat in the office after supper and had a little whiskey. He said what Beale did didn't make any sense to him."

"What about Beale?"

"Well, I don't know, Jim, except that the officer told me he was goin' to tell his commander that maybe he'd ought to be replaced." Glover stepped up to fling his near-side stirrup-leather over the saddleseat and loosen the latigo. As he was doing this and had his back to Campbell, he said, "How's

Miz Turner and the lad?"

"Fine . . . Henry, Joe was tellin' about a nice little dappled gray horse Hickson has down there. You know anything about him?"

Glover turned. "Yes, as a matter of fact I do. Bud bought him for peanuts from some starved-out homesteaders. He's a real quiet, nice horse — but not heavy enough for cattle work."

"Gentle, is he — you know that for a fact?"

Glover bobbed his head. "I know he's gentle. I saw three of those settler-kids all riding him at one time without no saddle an' usin' a cotton rope for a bridle. But he's not stout enough — "

"I don't want him for the ranch, Henry. I want him for Wes," stated Campbell, and squinted into the distance. "Him and Mary Jane drove out in the top-buggy awhile back to look at the wild flowers. The boy should have somethin' to ride that won't buck him off or run away with him."

Marshal Glover liked this idea. "He never bucked in his life, Jim, and he wouldn't run off if you set a firecracker under him. . . . How's Miz Turner takin' to ranch life?"

Jim Campbell jerked his head. "Come on over to the house. It's goin' to be hot out here directly." As they strode side by side Campbell continued, "She's taken to it like a duck to water. . . . Henry?"

"Yeah."

Campbell cleared his throat and led the way up to the porch and through the house to the kitchen. As he pointed to a chair for his guest and went rummaging in a cupboard for two glasses and a bottle, he said, "You ever been married?"

The big, burly peace officer looked startled. "Well . . . once, when I was young. She died of the cholera."

Campbell put the glasses down with the bottle and pulled out a chair. As he sat down he looked only at the tabletop. "Tell me how you did it?"

Campbell was pouring so Marshal Glover watched this as he replied. "Did what?"

"Got her to marry you."

Glover raised his eyes. For a while he was silent as he pulled the glass inward, then he said, "You ask, that's all."

"No, damn it, that's not all. How do you spark them? I been wearin' clean shirts and kickin' the dung off my boots before I come inside, and shaving every day and — "

Glover started laughing. Campbell glared at him. Glover restrained himself and held his glass up. "Good luck, Jim." They sipped, then Glover put his glass down and leaned forward looking very serious. "That's a fair start, shavin' and cleanin' up and all, but you got to . . . Don't get mad at them. Even if you do, bite your tongue. And when you go to town, fetch them back something; some calico or gloves or maybe a hat from the general store."

Campbell was listening as he leaned on the table. "That takes awhile, don't it?"

Marshal Glover nodded his head, shrewd eyes on the older man. "It takes awhile. Jim, did you ever break a horse just right without it takin' awhile, or maybe kept back quality heifers to upgrade your stock and had to wait a year for 'em to calve?"

Campbell did not reply. He sipped more whiskey and sat loosely, gazing across the table. "Did you know I was married once?"

Glover hadn't known. He'd heard faint rumors but had never believed them. "No. If you was, then you know how to — "

"No, I don't know. She was a Ute woman. I gave her paw horses for her. . . . Henry, this isn't the same at all."

Glover had to agree with that. Anyway, there wasn't anyone to give horses to for Mary Jane Turner, unless it would be her brother. At the thought of that Glover wanted to laugh again but knew better, so he drank some whiskey instead. It had been a long ride out and a long time since he'd had breakfast. Malt whiskey would creep up on an empty man, even when he was sitting down. Glover pushed the two-thirds empty glass aside, looked around the immaculate kitchen, then back to his host.

"That officer said something about a Mister Hawk. . . . Was that the old devil who is the boy's grandfather?"

"The same, Henry. Gus caught him in the mountains. Mary Jane cut his hair and I put an old suit of mine on him. He looked almost civilized."

"Where is he now?"

"Went back up to Spirit Meadow yesterday. . . . I gave it to him. Spirit Meadow, I mean. We'll finish gatherin' directly, then go up and build him a log house."

"I didn't know you owned the meadow, Jim."

"Owned it for forty years but never used it," replied the old cowman. "I asked my new rangeboss, Joe Bryan, if he knew why I didn't graze it off and he said because there were varmints and predators up there. I told him he was plumb right."

"Well . . . "

Campbell's shrewd eyes rose to the other

man's face. "You don't believe in ghosts and whatnot do you?"

Marshal Glover shook his head even though he was now looking straight at two James Campbells when he knew perfectly well there could only be one of them.

Campbell continued speaking. "I do, Henry. That's why I haven't gone to that meadow in forty years. They're up there. . . . No, now wait a minute. You never was up there when the moon was full. Three times I climbed into my bedroll up there and each time the old man I gave those horses to for his daughter started talkin' inside my head, plain as you an' I are talking."

"What did he say?"

"He give me hell. One of those horses went lame, another one got foundered, and another one couldn't be rode."

Marshal Glover eyed his glass but remained resolute and did not touch it. He sighed, looked at James Campbell and said, "All right. Now tell me — did your Ute woman talk to you too?"

Campbell finished his whiskey and remained clear-eyed and clear-minded. "No, an' that was another thing the old man give me hell about. He said she couldn't. People that take their own lives can't come and talk."

Marshal Glover reared back in his chair. "An' you don't like it up there?"

"No, I don't."

"You told me you were goin' up to build old Hawk a log house."

"I didn't mean *I* was goin' to build it, Henry. I'm goin' to send Joe Bryan and a couple of other men. They'll build it."

Glover squeezed both eyes closed then sprang them wide. "How is Bryan workin' out?" he asked, to change the subject.

"Just like I thought he would," replied the older man. "He's good with livestock. He gets along with the men — which ain't always easy. Gus Acosta, for instance, isn't the easiest man to work with, but he's the best man with horses I ever saw."

That reminded the lawman of something. "The last man you hired — some folks in town said he looked like the picture in the newspapers a few years back of that feller who robbed stages — Wood Griffin."

"That's who he is," stated Campbell. "Henry, in your business a man's past is important. In my business it don't mean a thing if he's easy to be around, can rope halfway decent, can shoe horses and ain't lazy. Griffin's a good hand — and don't you get to chousin' him when he comes to town."

Marshal Glover was agreeable to that although he did not say so. He would not have had a chance to speak if he had intended to. Campbell looked stonily at him. "What did you do with those horsethieves?"

"Nothing yet. That blasted circuit ridin' judge hasn't come to town. But they'll wish he hadn't when he gets here. If there's one thing that cranky old man don't like it's horsethieves."

Campbell looked pleased about that and leaned to pour more malt whiskey into the lawman's glass, but Glover was too quick for him; he covered the glass's top with a palm the size of a small ham. "I got to ride back to town," he exclaimed, shoving back the chair to stand up. "What kind of whiskey was that, anyway?"

They went out to the porch. The heat had finally arrived and it would continue to build up for the balance of the afternoon. Glover hesitated to ask a question before walking down across the yard. "The old man Hawk; seems I remember hearing the army wanted him pretty bad."

"Half a century ago," replied Campbell, leading the way to the tierack down in front of the barn. "He was scairt peeless when those soldiers rode into the yard with Frank Beale.

I told him the soldiers wouldn't know about him. They wasn't even born back then, and besides I told them his name was Mister Hawk, not Aaron Love, like it'd be in their old records."

Glover watered his horse and cinched up, hitched at his britches then struggled up into the saddle. "You never did tell me what kind of whiskey that was, Jim."

Campbell looked up a little critically. "Malt whiskey. The best a man can buy. It come all the way from Denver wrapped in straw with only one busted bottle. Trouble with you, Henry, is that your insides are used to that popskull they sell in Springville. . . . Now, you hang on ridin' back, you hear me? And ride slow."

Marshal Glover turned out of the yard with Manuel Lewis watching his progress over in the shadows of the cookhouse porch. After the lawman was gone he looked down where his employer was leaning on the tierack shaking his head, and called over. "Was he drunk?"

"Yes. On one glass of whiskey. I've known Glover a long time and that's the first time I knew he couldn't handle good whiskey. . . . Manuel, when'd Miz Turner say she and Wes'd be back?"

"Couple of hours . . . Good thing Glover left before she come back. Womenfolk just plain don't like drunks around."

"Manuel?"

"Yes."

"You ever been married?"

The cook straightened up very slowly staring at his employer. "No, I never been, an' if a man's got a lick of sense he'd never get into something like that."

"Why?"

"Well," the cook said, and waved his arms helplessly. "Just because."

Campbell nodded. "Yeah," he said very dryly and went back to hide the evidence of the drinking before Mary Jane and Wes returned.